JAKE'S TEMPTATION

Parker Ranches Inc., Book 6

Maddie James

Copyright © 2017, Maddie James
Jake's Temptation
eBook ISBN: 978-1-62237-492-2
Print ISBN: 9798201117764
Originally published as *Good Enough*, an Amazon *Hell Yeah!* Kindle World book, 2017
Re-release by Maddie James, August 2018; revised and updated 2020.
Editor, Deelylah Mullin
Cover Design by Jacobs Ink, LLC
All rights reserved. The unauthorized reproduction or distribution of this copyrighted work, in whole or part, by any electronic, mechanical, or other means, is illegal and forbidden.

This is a work of fiction. Characters, settings, names, and occurrences are a product of the author's imagination and bear no resemblance to any actual person, living or dead, places or settings, and/or occurrences. Any incidences of resemblance are purely coincidental.

This edition is published by Maddie James, Sand Dune Books, Turquoise Morning, LLC, dba Jacobs, Ink, LLC. PO Box 20, New Holland, OH 43145.

Acknowledgements

And as always, mega thanks to my awesome editor, Deelylah Mullin.

JAKE'S TEMPTATION

Parker Ranches Inc., Book 6

Mira Featherstone knows her place in life and it's not with Jake Remington. Rich guys play on the wrong side of the tracks, but they don't bring girls like her home to mama. Since Mira has no expectations beyond the moment, she doesn't mind playing—and she loves toying with the bad boy lawyer, until it gets her into trouble with her boss, Chandler West.

Jake Remington is a wealthy Texas cowboy whose family land borders West Hills Ranch, owned by Chandler West. Although he now practices law and lives in Kentucky, he is back in Texas to settle a land dispute between his parents and the Wests and plans to take care of business and get the hell out of Dodge before he gets himself into trouble. Again.

Because trouble for Jake always comes in the form of a Texas beauty, and one he can't keep his hands off. His last temptation landed him with a lawsuit.

But when he bumps into the flirty Mira coming out of his hotel room at the West Star Lodge, keeping his hands off the hotel maid becomes an impossible task.

Chapter One

"I am so damn sick and tired of cleaning up other people's shit and making their beds I could scream. Why can't they make their own damn beds? I bet they make them at home. Why not here?"

Mira Featherstone jerked back the bed cover and let the flimsy fabric float to the carpeted floor. Next, she swiped at the bottom, fitted sheet, and smoothed it out with her hands, evening out the indentations where someone must have laid all night long, not moving. How could people sleep like that? She was all over the bed.

That done, she straightened the top sheet, tucking it tightly back between the mattress and box springs, making sure to square off the corners. She hauled the bed cover back up over the bed neatly, then fluffed and placed the pillows.

There. She did good work.

Good enough for a nice tip, she hoped.

Glancing about, Mira wondered who was staying there. She generally knew which guest was in what room at the lodge, but she had been off for three days, tying up loose ends at her other job, so she was a bit out of touch. She glanced at the pair of boots in the corner. A man, she deduced, and alone. The bed was not messed up enough for two.

And no sex, obviously. At least if he'd had sex, he hadn't used the bed.

She could sure wreck a bed during sex. Sending sheets and pillows flying....

Not so this guy, obviously.

She sighed, trying not to think about sex—and the fact that she'd been without that particular pleasure of late—gathered up the small trash can by the desk, then headed toward the cocked-open door.

About the time she reached for the handle, it swung forward, sending her sailing backward on her ass. When she regained her faculties enough to see a large man reaching down to help her up, she realized she was utterly and completely in lust.

Holy mother of all things sinful. The guy staring back with his hand outstretched represented nothing short of cowboy crack. She knew if she partook of him once she wouldn't be able to stop, and that was the last thing she needed right now. Her gaze traveled upward, perusing every God-given feature the man possessed—deep-set black eyes, chiseled chin and cheek bones, and a scruffy five o'clock shadow that could probably be a beard in a couple of days. All of which were perfectly set below a black, straw Resistol, cocked sexily to one side. Her gaze traveled down the center placket of the man's starched, white button-down collared shirt, outlined by the lapels of a black suit jacket. His entire look was polished off cowboy style with a wide leather belt sporting the prettiest silver and turquoise buckle she'd ever seen, dark blue Wranglers that appeared to stretched tight over his ample crotch, and a pair of black caiman boots she knew for a fact cost a whole lot more than her month's salary.

Holy shit. Her clit tingled already. She grasped his hand and he hauled her up fast, her chest bumping his, her nipples suddenly on fire. Up on her tiptoes, their gazes connected and held while he said in a fathomless voice that rivaled the depth of his eyes, "Sorry about that, miss. My bad."

She nodded. "Yes, you are."

He cocked a brow. "Excuse me?"

"Bad. That. You." *Shit.*

She broke away and looked toward her feet where the trash can had dumped and strewn the badass cowboy's crap all over the floor. She bent to pick up the stuff, uneasy with the guy towering over her. Empty cigarette pack. Soft drink can. Crumpled napkin. Condom wrapper.

Gulp.

She looked up. He reached down, scooped the items up, and placed them in the can. He sat it on the floor. "There are some things a lady just shouldn't have to pick up," he said.

Mira wanted to melt into a puddle on the floor. Lady? He obviously didn't know her reputation. Could she disappear right now? No. Because of his eyes. Still. Looking into hers.

Holding her to him.

"Um, thank you." She finally managed to pull her gaze away. "I'll come back and finish the room later."

He grasped her elbow and she glanced back. "That's not necessary," he said. "I'll only be a minute. You live around here?"

Mira gulped again and nodded. "Yes. I mean no. I mean, I'll come back later." She stepped through the open door, paused, and glanced back. "It's...protocol." Then she turned and pushed her cleaning cart down the hall toward the next room. Fast.

"No need to rush off on my account, little lady," the voice behind her said.

Oh yes there is, the voice in Mira's head echoed. *Plenty of reason.* Like, she didn't want to be fired for cavorting with the guests. Again. Chandler West had made himself quite clear after the last time. One more slipup and her employment at West Star Lodge was over. She needed this job so—

As much as she would like to jump Mr. Cowboy Crack's bones—right here and right now—he was off limits. And as soon as she finished in room 203, she'd find out how long he was here for and would avoid him like the plague. Even though what she really wanted to do was ride him like the mechanical bull she rode once at a bar in Kerrville.

Jacob Remington watched the girl slip into the next room down the hall. *Girl nothing.* She was a full-blown woman and one who was not only easy on the eyes, but also possessed enough curves and dips for his oversized cowboy hands to grip and fondle with ample flesh left over. His kind of woman. Thick and luscious—plenty of spots for his tongue and cock to explore. And before this week was through, he planned on doing just that—bury himself so deep within her soft curves and crevices he'd never wanted to come out.

Hell. What was he thinking?

It was that kind of reckless mindset that got him into trouble the last time he visited Texas. The three decadent nights he'd spent with one of the local girls had turned into a nightmare and a lawsuit. Turned out the girl was pregnant but not by him. Thank God for DNA. Thing was, though, it *could* have been him—he'd been careless enough that it scared the shit out of him ever since.

He glanced down to the condom in the trashcan. Thank God, he'd finally matured enough sexually and realized the consequences. You'd think one would have learned those kinds of lessons by age thirty-two, right?

Well, he guessed he was a little slower than others.

Not him. When it came to women—especially beautiful, voluptuous women like this one—his brain sailed out the window and all he thought with was his dick. Of course, he and his dick had had a lot of fun over the years, but it was time to be more responsible.

After all, he was a professional man. A businessman. He couldn't afford to be a horny bastard forever, could he? One day, for certain, it would come back to bite him. And not in a good way.

His thoughts rolled back to the woman he'd met up with in the bar last night. He hadn't been cautious in the least, but he had used a condom. Hell, she was hornier than he was, and they never even made it to the bed. Just divorced, she was eager to bury the memory of her ex-husband in tequila and cock. He'd fucked her up against the wall in his room and it was all over in ten minutes—with seconds to spare, likely.

Embarrassed afterward, she'd straightened her skirt and cleaned up quickly in the bathroom. He'd walked her down to the lobby and had the desk clerk call her a cab. It was an uncomfortable twenty minutes until her ride arrived, but she'd thanked him and turned away hurriedly, leaving him standing alone.

This morning, he couldn't even remember her name.

It was for the best. Her emotions were too raw and his were permanently disconnected from sex. Sex was sex, nothing else. Sex didn't equal love, relationship, or anything close. It was simply for the sake of getting off. Even though she echoed the same sentiments last night, he didn't think she was quite on the same page as him. He'd almost felt sorry that he'd nailed her—last thing he needed was an emotional nut case on his hands—but she'd come on so damn strong in the bar and had assured him she was ready to get on with her life.

Well, maybe. Maybe not. That's for her to figure out.

He stared down the hall at the housekeeper's cart. He'd take a helluva lot longer with a woman like the chick next door, if given half the chance. His cock started to rise to the occasion.

Dammit.

Shaking his head, he tucked back into the hotel room and searched for his cell phone, spotting it on the dresser. He'd left it there, he guessed, when he'd gone downstairs for breakfast. Time to switch gears and get his head off sex and the woman in the next room. He had work to do. He snatched up the device and swiped the face. Two missed calls and three texts. He'd read them while heading to West Hills Ranch.

Chandler West was going to be pissed with him for being late. What Chandler didn't know, though, was that he was going to be pissed at Jake for a lot more than that.

Mira listened to the heavy footsteps fade as they moved down the hallway toward the stairs. Good. He was leaving. She'd finish this room, and then quickly move back to his, before heading down to the desk and talking with Madeleine at the front desk. She wanted to know who the hell this man was and exactly why he was here!

It mattered. People didn't come to the West Star by happenstance. Oh, of course, it was a vacation spot, with the lake nearby and everything, but the hotel staff was made up of locals and everyone knew each other. There were regulars, of course, who came from out of town, too. But usually there were hometown connections and all she had to do was figure out this man's link to the area.

Snapping her fingers, she jogged to the window and scanned the parking lot. Vehicle. What type would he drive? That would tell her a lot.

There he was, strolling out from under the entrance canopy toward the parking lot. He passed the silver Mercedes and a couple of Harleys, then strolled by various and sundry dusty ranch vehicles, and finally headed for a late model, slick and shiny, candy-apple-red Dodge Ram dually pickup truck. A man's truck, that was for sure. Ranch truck? Maybe. But, too clean. This ride was slicker than pig's shit and darned fancy.

Maybe it was a rental.

No. She didn't think so. *Why rent a dually unless you were going to haul something and pull a trailer?* This guy wasn't hauling or pulling—and he was a guest at the lodge. She'd have to think about that.

He must have money. Shiny new truck without a speck of dust. Fancy belt buckle. Expensive jacket and Resistol. Damn expensive boots. Tony Lamas, maybe? She usually knew her boots.

She pondered that, too, while she watched him back up and pull straight-ahead then toward the road. Watching him from afar made her clit throb even more. Involuntarily, she reached between her legs and squeezed. She should get a grip, but she would love to get off right now thinking about him.

No. Not here. She watched as he turned left and rolled down the highway. She wondered where he was heading and clicked off the possibilities in her mind. Once he was out of sight, she turned back toward the room and aimlessly worked to finish cleaning room 203.

But her mind drifted.

She glanced at the wall this room shared with 201, her brain tripping over recent, and very interesting, turn of events. Mr. Cowboy Crack was likely the finest looking stranger to invade these parts in some time. And even though he was hands-off, she could still fantasize about the man, couldn't she?

Of course, she could. Fantasies were personal and untouchable.

Her eyes closed and she replayed the few minutes she'd spent with him in her head. Thinking about it nearly sucked the breath right out of her lungs. She mentally perused his body one more time. Black hat, white shirt, tight jeans, black expensive boots...

Total package. She imagined his *package* was totally fine, too.

Chapter Two

Jake pulled up to the main house at West Hills Ranch. Taking a deep breath, he stepped out of the truck, then turned back to grab his portfolio off the passenger side seat. Tucking that under his arm, he slammed the truck door and headed up the steps to the veranda, crossed it and pushed the doorbell. The tone echoed through the cavernous entry of the Texas ranch home. The style of the home was more antebellum than Texas ranch, and he'd heard it was because West was originally from the tri-state area with family in Louisiana. His wife, Celine, was a born-and-bred Texan, and he could see her influence in the home too. The couple and Chandler's brother, Brice, bought the land several years ago. Where West and his brother got their money, he wasn't certain—hard work was what Chandler always said—but no matter how, they were making a big splash in the rancher world regionally.

He respected that, them being relative newcomers and all. Hard work paid off in dividends. But with Jake growing up in Hill Country, on a ranch that his family had owned for a couple hundred years, he was not quite as trusting of the West's as some of the others in the area. The Wests still had some dues to pay—in his book, anyway.

He heard the sharp click of boot heels on the hardwood flooring before the door swept open and Chandler West greeted him.

"Jacob. Good to see you. Come on inside," Chandler said, then added, "Can't imagine what brings you back to Texas. Kentucky lost its appeal?"

Jake crossed the threshold and put out his hand. "Not at all. I love living in Kentucky, but Texas will always be home. I have a little business to take care of here for my parents—not to mention spending a little time with you. Thanks for seeing me, Chandler. I apologize for being a few minutes late. I promise I'll be brief."

Chandler eyed him, a little too suspiciously, Jake sensed. Then Chandler's face broke into a smile and he took Jake's hand. "No problem. I am curious why you're here but I'm sure we'll get to that." He motioned to a room across the hall. "Let's step in here. Can I get you anything? Coffee? Whiskey?"

Jake grinned. That whiskey question was a bit of a dig. He remembered the last time he had visited his parents and caught up with the Wests at a local hangout. He and Chandler's brother, Brice, had gotten into a hell of an argument over the finer points of whiskey versus bourbon. Of course, Jake could spin those finer points of bourbon all day long. And Brice, the same with whiskey. It had been an interesting night of trading shots and seeing who could tell the bigger fish tail.

Jake smiled. "A little too early in the morning for *bourbon* but I thank you all the same." He headed toward a leather chair sitting behind a large mahogany desk. This looked to be either Chandler's office or a study. "Mind if I sit here?" He placed his portfolio on the desk and opened it, then laid a hand on the back of the desk chair.

Chandler cocked his head, as if he'd caught on to Jake's game. "Go right ahead. I'll just sit over here." He stepped toward a leather chair to the left of the desk, which was precisely what Jake had wanted him to do. Jake wanted the upper hand and the power position. He also wanted distance between them.

Frankly, he was surprised Chandler acquiesced so easily—but then again, he had no knowledge of why Jake asked for this meeting.

Jake sat and rifled through a few papers.

Chandler tented his hands across his abdomen and stared at Jake, his face set and his lips thin. "Something mighty big must be brewing in order to pull you away from that little dynasty you've supposedly built up north in Kentucky."

Supposedly. Jake ignored that. "No dynasty, that's for sure, but I'm comfortable." He cleared his throat. Time to get down to lawyer business. "You know my parents' ranch borders West Hills Ranch to the south."

Chandler nodded. "Yes, I do."

"And you know that ranch has been in my family for nearly two hundred years."

Chandler nodded again. "Yes. I know that too."

"Great. Now, I know you've been around here long enough, but to some people you and your family are still considered to be...outsiders. Your roots don't run deep enough here yet, and so that makes some people a little bit leery of things."

Chandler cleared his throat and leaned forward. "What are you saying, Remington."

Jake pulled a letter out of his portfolio and slid it across the desk toward Chandler. "The ranch owners in these parts have been really lax on boundaries over the past hundred years or so, as you know. If we keep our livestock and our buildings and ranch hands where they belong, everyone is good. But some of your neighbors have a growing concern about things slowly inching out from your property onto theirs, and they would like for you to look into a few things."

Chandler left the letter sit on the desk. "Such as?"

Jake nodded. "It's all spelled out there." He rose and tapped his forefinger twice on the paper. "Now, if you have any questions, feel free to call me on my cell phone. It's there on the letterhead. I'll be here all week."

Chandler glanced at the letter and stood. "You mean to tell me you came all the way down here from Kentucky to deliver a goddamn letter?"

Jake nodded. "Yes. I could have mailed it. I felt I should deliver it in person. Now, I want you to read and think about the contents and then call me later. I'm staying at the lodge. I'll be visiting with some friends and family throughout the week, but I'm available to discuss anytime it's convenient for you."

"My lodge?"

Jake gave him a stare. "You own the West Star now?"

Nodding, Chandler said, "I do. I bought it a few weeks ago. Do you have an issue with that?"

"Of course not. I just didn't realize it."

Chandler took a couple steps around the desk. "Just mind yourself while you are there, Remington. I'm curious though, why aren't you staying with your parents? Cramp your style?"

Jake grinned at that one. He knew where West was heading. "My style never gets cramped, Chandler. Where there is a will, there is a way. Fact is, if you really want to know, my parents are remodeling, and they are at their condo in Florida for the month. Besides, the accommodations at the—I mean, *your*—lodge are quite nice. I always enjoy myself immensely when I stay there."

"Oh, I know you do, and so does half the female population in this part of hill country."

Jake knew it was time to drill his point home and retreat. "It would be wise if you would thoroughly look into the matter, Chandler. I know you and your brother have many irons in the fire, so perhaps this is simply a matter of overlook. I'm sure you want to spend a little time investigating the issue at hand."

"Investigating?"

"Yes. I'm certain you may not be fully aware of what is going on. I'd advise you to read the letter and talk to your ranch hands."

Jake watched Chandler's face screw up. "I'll take advice from my own damn attorney, Remington, not from the one who represents the other side of the fence."

Chuckling, Jake smiled. "Good pun, Chandler. You always were a funny guy." He picked up his portfolio and turned to head toward the entryway.

Chandler's footsteps followed. "So, Remington, about you're staying at the lodge…"

Jake stopped and turned back. What now? "Yes?"

Chandler narrowed his gaze. "Well. Seems to me that the last time you stayed there, you got into a little bit of trouble, as I recall."

Fulling facing him now and squaring his body, Jake eyed Chandler. "Look, West. I'm not the enemy here. I came because someone else was going to, and I talked my parents and the other ranchers into letting me handle this rather than some jackass attorney from Austin or Dallas. Read the complaints and see if you can figure out what is going on. Then let's talk. I'm sure we can settle this like reasonable, professional people, without gun slinging or name calling, or bringing up past issues that have nothing to do with this issue. Now, I'm leaving." He exited into the front hallway.

Chandler followed. "Remington!"

Jake turned.

"I'll read the damn letter and get back with you. In the meantime, keep your dick away from any of my girls at the lodge, you hear me? Your reputation around here is shit at best, and I'm quite sure you don't want that past dredged up again if this thing goes to court."

Jake set his face and glared back at Chandler. "First, whether we go to court or not, is up to you. Secondly, I will not be on trial in any case. And third, where my dick and I choose to play is none of your business—be it your lodge or elsewhere—so back off or this thing could get blown out of proportion to hell and back." He took two steps closer to Chandler and peered into his eyes. "And I mean that sincerely."

With that, Jake turned on his heel and left.

Mira stood in room 201 trying to decide her next course of action. She been procrastinating coming back to this room. She'd cleaned 203 and 205 and 207 already—avoid finishing cleaning 201 she could no longer do. She needed to vacuum the cowboy's room and clean his bathroom—but what she wanted to do was snoop.

That was wrong and against every ethic in the housekeeper's handbook.

If she got caught, she'd lose her job for sure, and probably never work again in this county or anywhere around here. She couldn't have that. People depended on her—*her dad* depended on her—and she needed to pull her weight. But the temptation was strong.

Never mind, I can find out info at the front desk.

She whirled, headed to the bathroom, and within twenty minutes, had it spit-shined and polished to a sparkle. As she stuffed used towels and washcloths in her cart, and reached for her vacuum, she glanced back into the room. Boots. She'd have to move those boots, wouldn't she?

She pushed the vacuum inside and plugged it into the wall. No, she was not supposed to touch guest's personal possessions. She'd vacuum around them. But as she got closer, she became a little more curious.

She tried not to look at them as she moved the sweeper back and forth over the carpet. When she finally got to the corner, she shut off the machine and stared at the boots. Heaving in a deep sigh, she bent over and picked up one to inspect.

She rose and turned them toward the light coming in from the window.

Just like the man, those were one fine and fancy pair of boots. Matte black with an Apache design, and she'd bet her bottom dollar that if she looked at the label they'd be handmade by the Heritage Boot Shop in Austin.

Yep. There it was. The leather was smooth as a baby's butt and—

The hotel room door behind her shut with a bang!

Mira screamed and dropped the boot.

She whirled, eyes stretched wide, to see Mr. Cowboy Crack standing a few feet inside the closed door, his hands-on hips, staring her down.

She gasped. "I'm so sorry. My apologies. I was just scooting them over so I could vacuum and..."

She bent to grab the boots and positioned them back in the corner. With her left hand, she grabbed the cord to the vacuum and jerked the plug out of the wall. The floors were clean enough. Then, she rose and began winding the cord onto the vacuum. "I'm just finishing up sir," she said, not looking his way and concentrating on the cord. "I'll be out of your way in nothing flat."

He said nothing.

Mira straightened, still not looking at him, and pushed the vacuum forward as she headed for the door.

Except she couldn't get around him.

He stood solid. Unmoving. And slowly, she lifted her head.

For some reason, an unhurried but satisfying sigh exited her body as her gaze met his. He looked down, his expression emotionless, his face fixed. Her own chest rose and fell with her even breathing. She didn't think he was breathing at all.

Too many seconds passed.

Then he moved. Slowly, he skimmed her left arm all the way up to her shoulder with his fingertips, leaving a trail of goose bumps on her exposed skin. Mira stifled a shiver as his hand settled at her neck and he gently cupped and caressed her cheek. Mira fought the strongest desire to lick her lips and nuzzled more firmly into his palm.

She lost the battle.

Leaning in, she closed her eyes. The cowboy shifted and placed his other hand on her waist. Rotating her slightly, he walked her backward until her shoulders were flat against the wall. His hand at her waist moved around to the small of her back, where he pressed tightly into her, forcing her belly to align with his.

His fingers dropped to encase the column of her neck. She felt pinned to the wall, and the feeling sent delicious twitters of pleasure throughout her body.

Mira's eyelids fluttered open. She looked up into his face.

His gaze penetrated. "Holy fuck, you are beautiful," he rasped. His fingertips gently massaged her jawline, and then tipped her head to the side. He nuzzled closer, his mouth finding the tender spot on her neck beneath her ear and leaving a hot brand of wet kisses in its wake.

Mira's heart pumped wildly, her breathing quick and shallow. She loved the anticipation of sex. The foreshadowing of the titillation to come. How he would feel. What he would do....

The unknown excited her like nothing else.

She exhaled and pressed into him. The cowboy groaned and nibbled lower. He pushed back the opening of her dress and popped the top button, widening the area and exposing her breasts a little.

His mouth followed.

"You have tits to kill for." He raked his mouth over her tender flesh.

Mira gasped and whispered. "Your mouth is so damn hot."

"My cock is hotter," he countered. "Just fair warning." Pulling back, he peered deep into Mira's eyes. She knew she was about to come unglued. A few more seconds of this and she'd tackle him to the bed and ride him like the barrel racing cowgirl she wasn't.

While he watched her face, he unbuttoned two more buttons and spread the placket of the dress wide. Mira glanced down to her black push-up bra and her boobs spilling out.

The cowboy's gaze lowered too, and his hands snaked inside the cups of her bra, one right and one left, lifting her tits. "I want these."

"Suck me," she said softly. "Suck me all you want."

"Ah hell..." The man buried his face in her chest. Mira threw back her head and sighed. This was her happy place—with a man's face between her tits and his cock in her pussy. When all those things came together, everything else went out the window. All was well in the world. She closed her eyes as he drew a nipple into his mouth. She loved the sharp intake and squirmed with pleasure. So much flesh put off some men, but it didn't seem the case with this cowboy. When she found a guy who loved to play there, she was in heaven.

"Oh yes," she murmured, as he moved from one breast to another. Tugging, flicking with his tongue. He twisted her other nipple with this thumb and forefinger while he sucked harder on the first one. "Fuck," she hissed. "You're making my clit throb, cowboy...."

Without hesitation, he dropped a hand to between her legs, bunched up her dress, and clutched her pussy. Mira gasped. "Oh shit!"

Something clattered out in the hallway, then a sharp knock to the door, followed by a male voice. "Mira?"

Jerked out of her sensual place, Mira pushed the cowboy away, and he didn't fight her on it. "Yes?" Her gaze still connected with his, she worked to button her dress back up.

"It's John from the kitchen. I'm going to take these room service dishes down now so you don't have to worry about them."

Mira huffed out a breath. "Sure, John. That's fine. Finishing up in here. I'll be down in a minute."

"See you then."

"Sure." She straightened her housekeeper's dress and looked down over herself to make sure she hadn't buttoned herself up crooked. No, she looked fine.

Except she wasn't fine.

"I need to go," she whispered, looking up. Her small voice shook with the words. Why did he affect her so? Any why did she allow him to touch her? Suck her...

Damn.

"Don't go," he countered. "Please. You need to finish up in here. Remember?" He cocked a grin and reached for her. Mira dodged him, moving toward the door.

"No. I have to go. I'm sorry about this. I never should have started—" *Something I can't finish.* She edged past him to grab the vacuum cleaner. "I need to go now."

He stared while she dragged the vacuum cleaner back toward the door. Out of the corner of her eye, she saw him move quickly and turn away, as if he were yanking himself back to reality too.

"I'm sorry to have startled you earlier," he said.

Startled isn't the word. Mira stopped and looked back, holding his gaze. She needed to get out of there. A thousand random thoughts spun through her head. Thank God he didn't know who she was. She should ask for tomorrow off. Or to clean a different floor. Too dangerous to see him again. Might not be able to control herself next time. Hell, she couldn't this time. "I... It's okay. I need to get out... I mean, I need to finish my work and..." Finally, she broke that steamy, ultra-connected gaze between them, turned, and pushed the vacuum toward the door.

"Mira."

Awkwardly, she twisted back. "What?"

"It is Mira, right?"

"How did you know?"

"Nametag."

Her hand went to the plastic tag on her dress. *Shit.* "Oh. Yes. It's Mira."

"Beautiful name."

She swallowed, linking with his gaze again. She didn't know if she could get enough of those bottomless, sexy black eyes. "Thank you." Her voice was squeaky.

"Beautiful woman."

She sucked in a quick breath to still the butterflies having a heyday in her belly. "Oh, thank you. Again." She turned back to the door.

"Will you be working tomorrow, Mira?"

God help her. She glanced back, her hair swinging over her shoulder, and saucily grinned. "I might."

Jake stood in place for several minutes after Mira closed the door behind her. He inhaled deeply and let the breath out slowly. Outside the door, he heard her rattling about with her cart, and then seconds later, the annoying squeak of the wheels as she pushed it down the hallway. It sounded like she could have even been mumbling to herself.

The woman affected him. No doubt. And had him rattled.

Had he affected her in the same way?

That was obvious, wasn't it?

Her tanned skin was velvet to his touch when he'd skimmed his fingertips over her arm. He enjoyed like crazy raising the tiny chill bumps on her skin. Her cheek felt like butter in his palm, soft and pliable. But the single thing that turned his insides to mush was the moment she'd turned her face up to look into his eyes.

Those big, brown doe eyes. They connected—on some higher, or perhaps basic level—more intimately than he'd connected with a woman before, given such a brief encounter. She was hesitant. Unsure. He could tell that. But there was something about the way she looked at him. How she angled her head slightly coupled with the intensity of her stare. Her eyes were wide and round, full of expectation and anticipation. They bore deep into his, searching for something, it seemed. Probably something he couldn't give. Yet, he was drawn to them—to her—and stared deeply into their depths for what seemed like hours.

In reality, seconds.

Long enough for him to realize that he had to break the spell they were under and pull back, take a minute to think, retreat. He was successful in doing that but—

But when he called out her name, and she turned back to look at him again—her long auburn-tinted hair cascading into a waterfall of curls over her shoulders, her red-lipsticked lips stretching into a sassy smile—he suddenly didn't want things to end. He didn't want this brief encounter to be all they shared.

He'd had to do something, anything, to show he was interested. Right?

Normally he was bold and brash enough to simply make a move. This was different. Mira was different. Wasn't she? He *had* promised himself he was not going to be so impulsive and irresponsible.

Try to do this one right, Jacob, for once in your life. Be a gentleman.

Besides, there was this thing with West. As much as he didn't like heeding warnings from anyone or doing what any person said, Chandler West was right. He needed to keep his dick in check while he was here—and especially *out* of the chicks working at his lodge. Last thing he needed was anything close to another scandal. Warning heeded.

But he still wanted this woman. *Mira*. It was a beautiful name. He wanted like hell to jerk off right now just thinking about sucking her tits.

But no. He'd wait. She was worth waiting for.

And he'd wanted her to know he was interested—didn't want the chance to get to know her to slip out of his fingers. He had to know if she was interested too, in return. As if the lengthy gazes between them were not proof enough of that.

So he'd tossed out some bait. *Will you be working tomorrow, Mira? I might,* she'd said. *I might.*

There was some kind of hope in that. Wasn't there?

Chapter Three

"Where are you going off to in such a hurry?"

Mira glanced over her shoulder as she pushed her timecard into the box to clock out. Madeleine Flores watched her from behind the front desk of the lodge. Mira pulled her card and stuck it back in the correct slot. "Home, after I get groceries. I need to pick up a few things for Poppy."

"Oh, I see. How is he doing?" Madeleine turned to face her.

Mira shrugged. "Better. As good as can be expected, I think. Losing Mom, and him having that accident on the ranch a couple of months ago has taken its toll. He can't go back to work for a while either, not until his physical therapy is complete, so there is that stress too."

Madeleine frowned. "What's it been now? Six months since your mom passed?"

Mira nodded. "Closer to eight. Seems like yesterday. I still can't believe she's gone. I guess time flies when you are busy."

"And you've been really busy. Are you still working two jobs?"

Mira shook her head. "No. They let me go downtown. I was just a part-time reporter and a new company bought the paper. They turned over the staff and everyone is now full time. While I would have loved that, and to have had the benefits, I wasn't considered because I haven't finished my degree. My last day was yesterday."

"Ah, honey. I always enjoyed your little articles." Madeleine reached over to hug Mira. "You've had a bit of a rough year, dear. I'm so sorry."

"Yeah. A bit. I'm thankful to get more hours here, though. Thanks for going to bat for me with Chandler."

"Ah heck, sweetheart. You know Chandler likes you. You're practically his family. It's just that he is so business-focused and well, this is a lucrative business for him, so he has to make sure everything is on the up-and-up."

"Yeah. I get that." And she did understand Chandler's position. Still, she couldn't afford to lose this job. Her father needed and depended on her right now. She smiled at studied Madeleine. "Thanks for reading my stories."

"You do a nice job, Mira. Quite the storyteller! You write non-fiction that reads like a story. I love that. One day, you're going to be writing bigger and better things."

That made her day and she leaned in to give the older woman a hug. "Maybe." She shrugged. That was a dream. To publish a book one day. It was nice to hear that Madeleine enjoyed her words. Mira wrote a weekly 'slice of life' column called *The Back Gate* at the end of the paper. One of those 'last word' columns. And when they were in a pinch, she did some sports reporting on the side. She hugged her friend back. "Thank you so much."

Madeleine was the mother hen of the lodge. She only worked during the busy season, but she made it her business to see that the staff was happy. Older than most of them—in fact, probably close to the age of Mira's father—she felt it her business to give advice as well as provide a shoulder to lean on. Most everyone appreciated her and loved her for it.

And she'd never judged Mira. Not once. Not even when she got caught coming out of that guy from Houston's hotel room after hours, and when Chandler West threw a fit yelling at her in the breakroom. She was sure that Madeleine saved her job that day, even though the woman had never said as much. Someone had spoken up for her because Chandler was fit to be tied and was ready to send her out the door.

Whoever it was, Mira was grateful.

Madeleine pulled back and looked into Mira's eyes. "I heard some of the other girls talking about running down to Kerrville tonight to have a little fun. Why don't you go with them? I'm sure they won't mind. In fact, there's Victoria now. Oh, Tory?"

"Oh, Madeleine, no..."

"Now shoot, girl. A night out would do you good." She turned toward Tory, who was approaching. "Honey, did I hear you say a bunch of you girls were going into Kerrville tonight? Can you take one more?"

Tory smiled. "Now, Ms. Madeleine, you wanna go barhopping with us?"

Madeleine swatted the air. "Oh, hell no. But Mira here could use a night out and..."

"Oh sure, Mira!" Tory's face lit up. "I would love for you to come. Did you change your mind? This morning when I asked, you said you needed to take care of your father so—"

Madeleine burst in. "Yes, she wants to go."

"But—"

The older woman turned to look Mira. "Go. In fact, I made a big crockpot full of soup beans today and I can't eat them all by myself. I'll run some out to your Pop and maybe keep him company for a couple of hours. How about that?"

Mira blinked. "I guess that's okay. I'll make sure to tell him you're coming so he's expecting you."

"All right, Mira. If you think that's best."

"Yes. And...well, sometimes he's a little crotchety with the pain and all, so if he's not nice, don't take it personally."

Madeleine smirked a little. "I'm a grown woman, Mira. I can handle crotchety old men." She winked and fully smiled. "I'll just drop off the soup and if he's not in the mood for company, I'll skedaddle on home. That sound like a plan?"

Mira sighed, wondering if Madeleine had designs on her father. She had mixed feelings about that. "Yes. That sounds good." Knowing

Madeleine was heading out to the ranch made her a little nervous. "I sure do appreciate it."

"Well, it's settled." Madeleine turned to Tory. "She's going."

"Great!" Tory looked at Mira. "Can you meet us my apartment at seven?"

"I..." Mira swallowed. *What the hell.* "Sure. Thank you, Tory. I'm excited!"

Tory smiled and headed out the lobby door, throwing out a wave. "See you then! 'Bye Ms. Madeleine!"

Mira watched her go and then looked back. "What just happened here?"

Madeleine smiled. "Just go with it. You deserve a little fun."

One thing Jake knew as he pulled off the highway and into the parking lot at Armadillo's, was that he had to get out of that hotel room tonight. The bar at the lodge wasn't going to cut it, either. He didn't want to risk running into Ms. Divorcee, nor anyone else in the area. So, the ninety-minute drive to Kerrville fit the ticket.

He needed to be around people, and he needed to think. A shot or two of tequila would help. Normally when he was home in Kentucky—on his thoroughbred horse farm outside of Lexington—he drank bourbon. And not just any, but one of the smoothest and most expensive. He lived in the mecca of bourbon and horses—and for him, only the finest of both would do. Over the years he'd become quite the connoisseur of the distilled beverage, and he wasn't bad at picking out winning horses, either. His preference was for a bourbon out of a small distillery in Woodford County, not far from where he lived. None finer, in his mind.

But tonight, his drink of choice would be tequila. Shots, lime, salt, and all.

As he shut and locked his truck door, he tucked his keys into his jeans pocket and crossed the parking lot full of pickup trucks and Harleys. Nothing better than the raw electricity of a biker-slash-cowboy bar to get your mind off a woman. He entered and stood for a moment to let his eyes adjust to the smoky darkness. Once he got his bearings straight, and had perused the lay of the land, he picked his way through the crowd of bikers, cowboys, and the women who loved them—or rather, who lusted after them.

He really had no desire to be fresh meat tonight and made no eye contact with anyone as he crossed the floor. The scowl on his face would turn most people off, he imagined. Yet for some, it could be a challenge. Didn't matter. He was in no mood to brush off pickup lines and push away drunken cowgirls who were too young to be in a place like this, anyway. He was in the frame of mind for one thing, and one thing only.

Soon, he'd settled himself into a dark corner, had ordered his first round of tequila, and sat back to watch the crowd.

He didn't want a woman tonight. Not one in this place anyway. All he wanted was to sit there and drink—and fantasize about fucking Mira.

At half-past midnight, Mira's head felt fuzzy, but she was smiling. She'd had a great time with the girls and was so glad Madeleine has pushed her to go. "I had fun lots," she said to Tory, then giggled. Tory sat beside her in the driver's seat of her Chevy truck, the designated driver for the evening, and it was a good thing, because Misty and Chloe in the backseat were plastered and singing another round of "We Are the Champions."

"I'm glad." Tory smiled. "And I'm glad you are not as drunk as those two!"

"Just a teeny drunk. I'm cheap." She hiccupped. "I mean a cheap drunk."

Still smiling, Tory said, "I knew what you meant."

"Hey!" Came a voice from the backseat. "Are we going by Dillo's? This road goes by there. Let's pop in for one more."

Mira widened her eyes. "Oh, my gawd. I haven't been there since I rode the bull. It's wild there, though. Do we really want to?"

Chloe and Misty started chanting from the backseat. "Dillos! Dillos!"

Tory tipped her head. "At least they've stopped singing. What do you think?"

"True. But I have to be at work at six."

"Dillos! Dillos!"

Tory continued. "Me too. Just a quick stop? It's sort of fun to go there. Makes me feel all bad girl and wicked."

Mira laughed and shrugged. She wasn't driving so didn't feel it was her call. "Up to you, Tory."

"Well, we're here. Let's pull in. At the very least, I have to pee."

"Pee. Pee. Pee." The chant from the backset found a new topic.

"We're here, girls. Hold on."

A few minutes later, after hooking the backseat girls by the arms and stumbling them through the parking lot, all four women fell into the bar. Mira blinked against the low lights and smoke whispering against neon signs as a backdrop. The place smelled of cigarettes and whiskey—probably permeated into the wood floor and walls. Her gaze shot to a sign that pointed to the restrooms and she urged the girls that way.

"Let's all go pee," she said. "And no matter what, we stay together."

It took several minutes for the giggling duo to do their business while Tory and Mira waited. Finally, with some cool water splashed on their faces, mascara checked and redone, and some alcohol out of their systems, the backseat girls were ready to hit the bar, perhaps a scant more sober than when they walked in the place.

Maybe.

They entered the smoke-filled room, which was crowded beyond belief, and edged their way toward the back and up to the bar. The duo ordered a couple of beers and headed off to the dance floor. Tory, of course abstained, and Mira contemplated whether she wanted another margarita.

"Go ahead and get something, Mira. I'm driving, remember?"

"I know. I just don't want a hangover in the morning." *I don't want to look like crap when I go into work either.* Her thoughts immediately shot to the cowboy in 201.

Are you working tomorrow, Mira?

She needed to put him out of her mind. She shouldn't even care if he asked her if she was working because she was not going to have anything to do with the man. It was nice putting some distance between herself and the hotel tonight. She needed to get perspective on the mess she could get herself in, should she succumb to the likes of the sexy Mr. Cowboy Crack.

She glanced at the bartender. "Margarita on the rocks, top shelf, with salt. Thanks."

Turning, she chatted with Tory while she waited and watched the girls with a couple of rough-looking cowboys. "Let's keep an eye on those two."

"Seriously," said Tory. "Chloe gave us the slip last time we went out and I worried all night whether she got home okay."

"Well, that's the last thing we need—to lose her in this place."

"For sure."

"Margarita, Miss?"

Mira twisted back and smiled at the bartender. Reaching into her small purse, she pulled out a twenty and handed it to him. A big cowboy hand grasped her wrist.

"Put your money away little lady," the man said. "This one's on me."

"Oh no." *Hell no.* She was not falling for that line. She rotated back to look fully at the man, and gasped.

Shit. No.

Cowboy Crack, in the flesh. And what flesh it was too.

With a crooked, saucy smile, he peered into her eyes and slapped a bill on the bar. His gaze didn't leave hers while the bartender took the bill. "Oh yes," he countered.

Mira licked her suddenly dry lips, watching him lean lazily into the bar with his right hip. Like he owned the place. Which of course, he didn't. She couldn't quite remember who owned it and she really didn't care.

Her thoughts halted when the cowboy took her twenty out of her fingertips, folded it into a smaller rectangle, and tucked it into her cleavage. The backs of his knuckles lingered against her tits, and Mira involuntarily shuddered and leaned closer.

The cowboy added, "Fancy meeting you here, sweetheart."

Mira stepped back and his hand dropped to the bar. "You don't have to pay for my drink."

"I know I don't, Mira. I want to."

"I'm not sleeping with you."

He cocked a brow and that crooked smile was back. "Oh? I didn't realize that option was on the table."

"It's not. Just getting that out in the open. Guy buys a girl a drink. Guy thinks he's getting in her pants. Not happening."

The cowboy lifted her margarita off the bar and handed it to her. "Drink up. You might change your mind, sugar."

Mira rolled her eyes. "I don't know you."

"That can easily be remedied."

"You have a comeback for everything a woman says?"

"Generally. What are you doing here, Mira? You girls look a mite out of place, and you know that makes you a lot more vulnerable. Right?"

"Perhaps. These girls know their way around the bar scene though." She cocked her head. "As to what I'm doing here? Same thing as you, I guess. Nice to get away for an evening."

He nodded. "Roger that. So, on the off chance that you are looking for a little action, just thought I'd let you know that you need look no further."

Mira sneered. "You're sort of high on yourself, aren't you?"

The cowboy laughed. "Mira, honey, you have no idea."

"What's your name?"

"What?"

"Your name. You know mine but I don't know yours. Not fair."

"Jacob. But you can call me Jake. Most people do."

Mira shrugged. "I'm not most people. I like Jacob better."

He countered her shrug. "Suit yourself. But when I hear Jacob I think people are talking about my father. I prefer Jake."

He put out his hand. "Jake Remington. And you are Mira…?"

Mira stared at his hand. Jake Remington. *Remington Ranch. Holy fucking shit!* His family owned a huge spread on the other side of the West ranch. An old Texas family. Big Texas money. *Shit.* She'd known *of* Jake—he was older than her in school—but he'd left the area a few years ago…or so she thought. Was he back?

"Mira?"

"Oh." She shook herself and took his hand. He grasped it tight and tugged her closer. "Featherstone. Mira Featherstone."

Jake grinned. "Hello Mira Featherstone." He thought a minute. "Not related to Cain Featherstone, are you? The bronc rider?"

One corner of Mira's mouth went up. "One and the same. He's my Pop. Except he's not riding much of anything these days but a rocking chair."

"I'm sorry to hear that." Jake looked sincere.

She nodded. "Yeah, his body's pretty much broken."

"Well, I guess things like that happen."

"Yeah."

"So." Jake trailed a fingertip between her breasts. "Now that the introductions are over, let's get the hell out of here."

He leaned in protectively and placed an arm around her back.

Mira stopped him with one hand flat to his chest. "Um, no. Jake. I'm with my girlfriends and we stick together." She looked over her shoulder to Tory—who wasn't there. Scowling, she looked back to Jake.

"She's off dancing with some biker and the other two are in a booth in the corner hanging over two cowboys who are probably going to nail them before the night is through. Let me take you home, Mira. I'm tired of this place. I want to get to know you."

"But I need to tell Tory..."

"Text her. You can do it from my truck."

Shit.

"I don't know. I..."

Someone nudged Mira from behind and shouldered in between her and Jake. A big someone. Biker dude. Full leather, skullcap, and all. "This asshole bothering you honey? Because if he is..."

Mira saw Jake stand up straighter, his chest broaden. "We're fine, man. I have this covered. And we're leaving. Right sweetheart?"

Mira looked from the angry-looking biker to Jake and immediately decided where she felt the safest. She nodded. "Yes, I'm ready *sweetheart*. Let's go."

Jake gathered her close and circled an arm around her. He eyed the guy who didn't budge; they skirted him and moved toward the door. Jake leaned in and whispered in her ear, his breath hot against her skin. "Now that's my girl."

There were no words to describe how those words made her feel.

Happy? Conflicted? Frightened? Perhaps all the above.

His girl. Mira swallowed. No way in hell she'd ever be his girl. He might fuck her, but be his girl? Never. Texas money like the Remingtons might play on the wrong side of the tracks, but they don't take girls like her home to mama.

Chapter Four

Hell. What had he just gotten himself into?

Jake pushed the passenger side door of his truck closed after tucking Mira inside. As he ambled around the rear of the truck—the long way around—to the driver's side, he sucked in air. Holding that breath for several seconds helped him to focus. A little.

Before he reached for the door handle, he paused and exhaled. Slowly.

His cock ached. Was dying to be unleashed. He burned to bury himself deep inside Mira's pussy and grind into her until he made them both come hard and fast and often. And soon. But he'd promised himself he'd be a gentleman. Right? He'd be thoughtful. Careful, not careless. Responsible, not reckless.

His plan for tonight had been simple—to get out of that damn hotel room for the evening. He'd not wanted to see Mira but was preparing himself to see her again in the morning. He knew he would—he saw it in her eyes earlier today. All he wanted was to fantasize about fucking her.

He definitely did not expect to run into her tonight.

Now, here she sits in his truck. At his own invitation. Waiting.

"I wonder what's going on inside her head."

He didn't know if he could keep his hands off her. For a moment, he closed his eyes and mentally recalled her walk across the smoky room after she'd entered the bar.

That damn, red, skin-tight dress she wore sent his libido spiraling out of control. Every straight man's eyes in the room slowly rotated toward her as she sauntered through the haze. Her skirt hit her thigh-high, her waist nipped in neatly over her hips, her ample rear punctuated the look with an exclamation point at every hitch of her step. The scoop neckline plunged low over her breasts showing ample cleavage; her tits begged to spill out of a black push-up bra playing peek-a-boo beneath the red fabric. Her hair looked on fire as it fell in long, soft curves over her back and swung slightly with the sway of her hips.

Good God. He could have jacked off underneath the table just watching her walk. That's when he'd stood up, crossed the room, and claimed her before anyone else in the bar had the same idea. Hell no.

Get a grip, man. He couldn't wait outside the truck forever. She probably wondered what the hell he was doing, standing out there mumbling to himself.

Lifting the latch, he hauled his body inside and sat, closing the door behind him. Illumination from a streetlamp a few feet away gave him enough light to see her. Mira rotated and looked at him as he sat there. They stayed silent. His gaze traveled softly over her face and he took in her slightly worried expression—then fell to her chest, which rose and fell with even but measured breaths.

"I do talk big," he said. "But I would never hurt you. Or anyone. You look worried."

She took a deep breath and let it out. "I'm not worried. Well..." She paused, her eyes widening a bit and settling on his face. "Okay, I am worried a little."

"Why? Don't be afraid of me, Mira."

Her gaze fell. She started fiddling with her fingers on her lap. Jake watched as she worked them over, clasped and unclasped her hands. "I'm afraid of touching you," she said softly. "Of you touching me. I'm afraid I'll like it too much."

Jake laughed out loud and placed a hand over hers, stilling her fingers. Her hand looked so small beneath his. He liked the way he covered her up and wanted like hell to cover her body with his. Right now.

"Liking it too much isn't a bad thing, is it?"

She jerked and glanced out the windshield. "That was one intense moment we had back in the hotel this morning." She looked back into his eyes. "It rattled me a bit."

"Me, too." He nodded and grinned a little. "Yes, it was intense."

"I'm strongly attracted to you," she admitted.

His grin broadened. "That's a good thing. I feel the same."

"I really want you to fuck me and fuck me hard and long. In fact, I'm afraid if we do, I might not be able to get enough of you."

Jake laughed and leaned closer. "Now we're getting somewhere." Reaching out, he fingered a tendril of her hair. Like red silk. He tugged that strand, leaned in and whispered. "I want that too, honey. Like you wouldn't believe. I'm not sure *strongly attracted* is a right enough phrase. I'm not sure when I've felt so drawn to a woman. I have to have you." His lips nuzzled her cheek. "But I have to tell you, honey, and odd as it may sound, it's just not about sex with you. I want to get to know you, the person, too. You fascinate me and we've barely scratched the surface in getting to know each other. I want to scratch a lot deeper than surface."

Mira pulled back and stared at him for a moment. "Seriously?"

Jake grinned. "Seriously."

Shaking her head, Mira said, "Jake, as much as I'd love for you to scratch deeper, all I really want is for you to scratch my itch. Nothing more. If you think there can be more, then this was a big mistake. I shouldn't have let it go this far." She turned slightly toward the door, and then back to look at him. "Look, I'll just go back inside the bar and find Tory. I'll go home with the girls." She reached for the door handle.

Jake's hope fell flat. He put his hand on her arm. "Wait. No. Please, Mira. Stay."

Her gaze met his. "I should go. You want more. And I'm not—"

"Not what?"

She swallowed her words and clamped her mouth shut tight. He wanted to know what she was *not*, but he didn't want to push it, either.

"I'm not willing to give more." She tilted her chin up in defiance.

"Oh really?" He cocked a brow.

"Yes. Really."

Grinning, he tugged at her arm. "Mira..." he said softly. "Come here. I want you."

Good enough. That's what I'm not. Good enough for you.

Mira felt brave in the bar, but the moment Jake sat in the enclosed cab of his truck beside her, all her boldness slipped away, and she felt enormously vulnerable. Sexually speaking, that is. And another part was that he was—well, a Remington, of course. He took up way too much space in the big truck cab. Jake was larger than life and sexier than hell, and every pore of his body oozed potent testosterone.

Her thighs began a slow quiver, aching to know what he would feel like between them. If she concentrated on that thought long enough, she might be able to make herself come.

But what fun would that be, without him in real life?

She couldn't find out. If they had sex, and if Chandler West ever discovered they were together—after all he was still a hotel guest—he'd have her job and then where would she be? Besides, this was Jake Remington sitting beside her. She wasn't...good enough.

And that was that.

But no one was talking about forever here, right?

Well, he was talking about *more*. Scratching deeper than the surface. Whatever that meant.

Jake's breath feathered against her cheek. His gentle tug of her hair with his fingertips made her lose sight of all reasoning. She was a lost cause. Jake Remington was a magnet, and she was drawn to him like a chunk of raw steel.

"Come here, Mira," he repeated. His lips grazed hers.

"So, we're not at the hotel," she whispered. "Right?"

He drew back. "I'm not sure what that means but no, we're not at the hotel."

"Or anyplace close."

"Honey, we're still in Kerrville, almost a couple of hours away."

"And no one here knows us."

"Except for your friends but I think they are probably occupied."

Mira knew Jake had no clue where she was going with this. "Then no one will know."

He tipped his head sideways a little. "Honey, if you don't want anyone to know we're together, my lips are sealed."

"Promise?"

"I don't kiss and tell. Besides, what happens between us is our business. No one else."

"And we're not talking about anything other than tonight. Right? We're just scratching itches here."

Jake eyed her. "Is that what you want?"

"Yes. Yes it is."

He blew out a breath of acquiescence. "All right, then. I agree."

She laid a hand on his crotch. "Okay. Then fuck me Jake Remington. Right here. Right now. Before I change my mind." *Before I lose my mind.*

He growled and the sexual stirrings inside Mira swirled and heightened. His hands went to her waist and he hauled her up on him. She straddled his thighs, her short dress inching up her to her hips. "Thank God you have tinted windows." Her words came out on a breath.

"Thank God I finally get to be inside you. Feels like I've waited forever."

Mira laughed. "It's only been, what? Fifteen hours or so since we met?"

He nuzzled her neck and Mira loved the feeling of his five o'clock shadow scraping against her skin.

"Feels like an eternity. Let's move to the back," he added. "I want plenty of room to properly fuck you."

Mira glanced into the extended cab of the pickup. There was a bench seat back there. Perfect. "Yes."

She separated from him and squeezed her ass through the front seats and into the back. Jake took the easy route, exited the cab, and came in the door. "Well, that was smart," she said and smiled.

He locked the doors with his key fob and tossed them into the front seat. "I'm a smart guy," he returned. Then he pushed her back against the seat and covered her with his body. "Smart enough to lure you into my lair," he added.

Mira giggled. "Oh, that sounded wicked."

"You have no idea, sweetheart."

"Show me."

"You're quite the tart, aren't you?"

"I've been holding back. Wait and see."

"And a tease, too."

Mira reached between their bodies and cupped his crotch. "And either you have a banana in your pocket or…"

"Oh, I'm incredibly happy to see you, Mira. Ecstatic. In fact, when I saw you in that bar, my every fantasy had finally been fulfilled."

"You're incorrigible."

"No, I'm insatiable," he countered.

"Sounds like we were meant for each other."

"Oh honey…" Jake growled again. "I do love a challenge."

A sensual thrill tripped over Mira's body. "Not much of a challenge here, Jake. If you haven't figured it out yet, I'm easy-peasy. A sure thing."

Jake smiled, then laughed. "Honey, if you were easy-peasy, I would have had you this morning in my hotel room."

She didn't have a snappy comeback to that, but it didn't matter. In seconds, she forgot the entire conversation.

In one motion, Jake skimmed his hands up her thighs and over her hips, moving her form-fitting dress up to her waist with his hands. He bypassed her thong and her belly and pushed her dress higher, the stretchy, sheer fabric giving nicely to expose her breasts. A half-second later Jake found the front closure of her bra, released her flesh, and buried his face between her tits. With his hands on each side of her boobs, he squeezed and smashed them into his face.

"Ah, shit," came his muffled voice. "Your tits have haunted me since this morning."

Mira shifted to wrap her legs around his hips and her arms around his back to hold him close. From somewhere inside her came a deep sigh. Holding him to her felt more than sexual—it just felt good, satisfying, and damn nice. After a moment, he surfaced and said, "I love your tits. I could play with them all night."

"Not too much?"

He pulled back. "God, no. Why would you say that? They're perfect."

She shrugged. "Most guys don't want more than a mouthful."

Jake squeezed her tits again, to where they were pushed tight and close together, her nipples hard and pointing at him. He licked from one to the other. "I'm not most guys."

Sighing, Mira relaxed and tipped back her head. "Oh, that's good, Jake. Really good. Play with me."

He didn't disappoint. Mira sank back into the truck seat while he squeezed and suckled at her breasts, teasing the hard peaks, going back and forth from one to the other. He drew her flesh between his lips, and she savored the wet heat of his mouth against her skin.

She groaned and arched into him, sensation diving directly to her clit.

"I love that," she whispered. "Don't stop."

Jake released a breast with a pop, leaned back, and tugged at her dress. "Here, let's get this all the way off."

Mira partially sat up while he peeled the dress over her head and she shrugged out of her bra. Jake's next movements sent his hands skimming down her belly and over her hips. "I love your curves. Every. Single. Fucking. One of them."

His hands on her body sent Mira into a spiral. As he inched closer to her clit, she anticipated the tremor he would quake within her, and longed for him to push inside her. But Jake had other ideas.

Spreading her legs apart, he flicked the thong aside, framed her pussy with his hands, and leaned in. Mira fully relaxed for a moment when his mouth covered her clit and started sucking. Immediately, tension built in her belly as he teased and flicked. Jake's tongue danced on her clit like magic and before long, she was on the edge of a powerful orgasm.

Jake must have sensed how close she was, wrapped his arms around her thighs, and hauled her up tighter against his mouth. Mira clutched at his shoulders and dug her fingertips into his muscles. Then, without warning, the orgasm ripped through her pelvis and exited out her curling toes, her head thrown back and pussy throbbing.

"God, Jake!" she shouted. The sensations rolled over her for a few more seconds and when she was nearly finished, Jake released her and drew back. In quick motions, he jerked at his belt and fumbled with his fly. Mira reached forward to help him push his jeans over his hips.

"Hold on," he whispered while fishing in his back pocket for his wallet. He produced it and a condom quickly, and Mira watched as he shakily ripped a corner of the packet off with his teeth and pulled out the rubber.

Mira grasped his cock and held it for him, realizing her own fingers were shaking. She was on the edge, needed and wanted more of him, and...something else. He affected her differently than other men. Being with Jake was just...different.

She watched Jake close his eyes at her touch. Condom securely rolled on now, he pushed at his jeans and again, Mira skimmed her hands over his hips to help. Jake wasn't to be denied for long, and obviously didn't care that his clothing didn't go very far.

"Just as long as they don't get in my way." He gasped the words.

Mira eyed him—his beautiful, erect, and thick cock—with anticipation.

Jake continued, "I can't wait any longer to fuck you, Mira. Goddamn I want inside."

He pushed her legs farther apart and pressed the head of his rock-hard cock against her core, sliding between her pussy lips, slowly edging deeper into her vagina. The sensation both thrilled and excited Mira. She spread her legs wider and squealed a little. He continued the in and out motion, working his way inside, until his body was flush with hers; his glorious cock filled her fully.

Mira whispered, "I want to suck you later. Want to fuck your cock with my mouth."

Jake groaned and ramped up his thrusts. Mira wrapped herself around him and held on. She reveled with his every plunge, his every tug and pull as he rocked her body. His length delighted her with its exit and thrilled her when it pounded back home again.

"You're so damn big, Jake," Mira hissed. "Give it to me hard and long. Don't you dare stop."

"Honey, I could live inside of you."

Mira shivered and dug her fingernails into the shirt over his back. She wished they were in a bed somewhere, fully naked, where she could explore all of him.

Touch all of him. She loved skin to skin. Friction.

Another time. This couldn't be the only time, even despite what she'd said earlier. Could it?

A low growl started deep in Jake's throat and the sound of his pending pleasure kick-started the hot pressure of another orgasm funneling up inside Mira's body. The angle was perfect as he rapidly nudged her G-spot and Mira felt her lower body unwittingly unravel and uncoil. She called out and threw her head and arms back. Jake grasped her hips and gave her several last hard and fast thrusts.

She exploded—and gasped out high-pitched, incoherent sounds.

He shouted out her name and pushed harder into her, then stilled. Mira's breath came in quick gasps as sensation journeyed up and throughout her body. Her hands went to her nipples, which were on fire, peaked and rigid like small pebbles. She played with them while watching Jake's face—his eyes closed, his brows knit, his breathing labored.

He collapsed over her. "Goddamn, woman. Hell. I'm sorry."

Mira laughed and hugged him. "For what, you silly cowboy?"

"For going too fast. For just fucking. I wanted to give you more attention. I wanted to make it last. I wanted—"

"Stop," Mira interrupted. "Just stop, Jake Remington. You were perfect. I came twice. You came damn hard. We're all good here."

He raised up then and looked into her eyes, studying her face for several seconds. "No. We're *not* good here. You're too good a woman to fuck fast and leave. I want you in my bed tonight, Mira. All night. Come back to the hotel with me and let me do this properly."

Too good a woman...

Mira blinked back the sting in her eyes. What could any woman say to that? She couldn't refuse. Against her inner gut warnings, she whispered, "All right, Jake. All right."

Jake drove with Mira curled up next to him. The damn console was in the way, but she made the best out of it. She leaned into his shoulder, dozing, while he drove. He kept one hand on the steering wheel and the other tucked in tightly between her hot thighs. Her hands were pressed over his wrist, holding him there.

It was a simple gesture, yet it turned him on like nothing else. His cock was rigid and ready again, and he hoped to hell he could hold his control long enough the next time. His plan was to make Mira hum all night long and by morning, she'd be warm and soft and pliable and hopefully...his.

He glanced to see the even rise and fall of her chest, her breathing soft. Auburn curls fell over her shoulder and spilled onto her breasts, held snugly in place by her bra and that damn skin-tight red dress.

Still, there was ample cleavage for him to ogle, and more. He couldn't wait to do more—and very soon.

He exhaled as the hotel came into sight. This woman beside him... This Mira. She was...

He couldn't explain it. All he knew was that every time he looked at her, every time their gazes connected, he was lost. And not just in a sexual way. There was more.

Yes. That was it. Mira was more.

More woman than he'd ever had in his life. And he loved the thought of that.

Chapter Five

The truck stopped and Mira jerked. She leaned up and away from Jake, brushing her hair out of her eyes, and looked at him.

He pushed the gearshift into park and reached for the keys to turn off the engine. Mira stopped his hands.

"Wait."

Jake stared at her. "Why?"

She glanced toward the hotel, and then blew out a breath. "Let's drive around to the other side. Come in the back door. Okay?" She couldn't afford to be seen coming in the front door with a guest.

Jake didn't respond and she glanced back to his face. "Please?"

"I don't understand."

She shrugged. "I work here. Right? It could be...complicated."

He tilted his head. "Ah. No cavorting with the guests, huh?"

Nodding, she replied, "Yeah. Something like that. Do you mind?"

He shook his head. "Not at all. Show me the way."

"Over there." She pointed to the right side of the building. "We can go in the door to the rear. Your room is up one floor and to the left. Easy-peasy."

"Like you." Jake laughed.

Mira grinned to herself and looked out the window. "Shut up and drive, Jake Remington."

"Yes ma'am," he returned.

In the room, the door locked and dead-bolted behind him, and the drapes pulled tight against the Texas sunrise that would no doubt penetrate the room entirely too early, Jake turned out one lamp, then another, while Mira stood by the bed. He left the light on in the bathroom behind him—just enough illumination filtering through so that he could see every curve of Mira's body, and every expression on her face—enough to soften the atmosphere and set a bit of a mood.

In all practicality, mood really didn't matter. All he wanted to do right now was make love again to Mira. The lighting wasn't important. What mattered was that they had the rest of the night, they had plenty of room, and they had each other.

Dammit. Listen to yourself Jake Remington. You're getting all sappy over a woman.

Damned straight. That, I am.

And for some crazy reason, he was okay with it.

"Come here," he whispered, and crooked a finger at Mira. "I want to hold you."

Mira stepped forward, almost shyly. She grasped his hand and he gathered her close into him, one arm circling her back, the other caressing her face.

"You are beautiful," he whispered. "I've been captivated by you since the first moment I laid eyes on you this morning." She tipped her head up and his lips landed softly on hers. Her mouth was soft, pliable, and warm. He dipped his tongue past her lips and probed inside, tangling his tongue with hers.

Mira made a little squeaky sound and he smiled and withdrew his tongue. Pulling back, he framed her face with both of his hands, brushing strands of hair away from her face. "I want you to know that I am captivated by you, Mira Featherstone. I'm not sure why or how it all happened so quickly, but I am."

Her eyes grew slightly rounder and she gave him a small grin. "I think that is a good thing?"

He nodded. "Very good. I just want you to know..." Dammit, should he even go there now? He wasn't sure but... "Mira, I really feel something for you. I don't want you to think that you're just another girl in my bed tonight."

She tilted her head and leaned back. "What?"

"You know. The condom you saw this morning. I... well, it happened. But this? You? Tonight? It's..."

"Different?"

He exhaled. "Yes. You make me feel different."

Mira's gaze played over her face. "Jake, whatever you did last night is none of my business. Just like anything I did last night is none of yours. This is just tonight."

Just tonight? But what if I want more?

Jake swallowed. Something stirred in his gut. Wait. "You did something last night?"

Mira grinned and cocked a brow. Then leaning in, she whispered, "None of your damn business, Jake Remington," she said, jerking at his belt. Slowly, she knelt before him, undid his buckle, and unzipped his pants. "I told you I wanted to do this earlier, right?"

She unleashed his cock into her hands. He looked down to see her looking up smiling, eye-level with his crotch. Her velvet fingers stroked up and down lightly and Jake couldn't help but close his eyes and just feel. After a moment, she took him into her hot little mouth—wet and slick—and he had to open his eyes and watch her take him deep. Her red lips stretched over his cock, sliding up and over his head.

He trembled. Literally, shook. "Jesus, Mira..."

Her big brown eyes looked back up at him, her tongue lapping at the side of his cock, then popping the head back between her lips.

"Sweet mother..."

Jake stood there and let her run her mouth all over him, taking his dick in deeper and sliding out again. He waited as long as he could, savoring the sensation rolling over him, but his legs were growing weak and the urge to come in her mouth was powerfully strong.

No. Not yet.

He reached for her. "Mira, come here." He grasped an upper arm and hauled her up so he could kiss her. Her breath was hot, and she was trembling. He fought the urge to throw her to the bed and just fuck the hell out of her.

Not this time.

He gently caressed her face with both hands, kissing her like she was his last breath. His last hope at life. At least a life that was meaningful and fulfilling in ways other than business deals and frequent-as-hell happenstance sexual encounters.

And maybe she was.

The thought of Mira being more to him sent a frenzy of emotion throughout his body—emotion he wasn't sure he knew what to do with, but also knew that he liked.

Mira was more. And he wanted to show her exactly how much she meant to him.

She fumbled with the buttons of his shirt and together, they quickly rid him of it, then jeans, boots, socks, and underwear. Jake kicked them aside and looked at Mira standing before him. She reached for the hem of her skirt.

He stopped her. "Don't. Let me. Turn around."

The dress was made to stretch and fit over her curvy form, almost like a second skin. There was a zipper in back, which he realized he had totally ignored earlier in the evening. Jake lowered the fastener inch by sinful inch revealing her beautiful, tanned back. He had to wonder if she sunbathed in the nude and hardened even more at the thought of ogling her from afar while she lay naked in the sun.

He smiled at that idea and spread the filmy fabric aside. Sliding his hands underneath the straps, he skimmed his hands down over her shoulders, peeling the dress lower as he did. He kissed down her spine, one gentle kiss at a time. One vertebra at a time. Skipping over the band of black fabric of her bra, he moved toward the small of her back. There, he lingered, tickling that sensitive area with his tongue, while the dress descended and settled at her hips.

Mira shivered slightly and sighed. Jake physically felt and heard her reaction.

He skimmed his palms over her curves and slid the dress south. It eventually fell to the floor revealing her ample derriere and a thin strap of black string arching over her hips and separating the crack of her ass. Mira stood before him in nothing but the thong and a lacy black pushup bra. Her ass was fucking awesome and he couldn't wait to bury himself there.

His hands went to her fleshy cheeks and he exhaled as he drew closer. He flicked at the string of fabric in his way and tugged the thong off her hips and down her legs. It dropped to the floor. Mira stepped out of it and started to turn around, but he halted her.

"No," he whispered. "Stay right there." He wanted her facing away from him.

Kneeling now, Jake massaged her ass with both hands. "Bend over a little, Mira," he said. "Put your hands on the bed and spread your legs a little."

She did and his libido zinged. Her musk, mixed with the scent of their earlier lovemaking, wafted toward him and hit him like a ton of bricks. He loved everything about this woman. How she felt. How she smelled. How she fit his body like a glove.

Jake spread her ass cheeks apart to reveal her luscious pussy. Knowing that he could probably never get his fill of her—and didn't want to—he pressed into Mira's pussy from behind, drawing her labia into his mouth. Being buried into her center not only thrilled him sexually but also gave him a heady feeling of possession.

He wanted her. All of her. And as his tongue found her clit, he flicked and rubbed over that firm bit of flesh he knew was the center of her universe right now. Knowing that he was doing everything in his power—consciously and perhaps even more subconsciously—to claim her, to inundate her with pleasure, that's all he wanted. Give her pleasure. Be her pleasure.

Yes. To claim her and make her his.

She moaned and trembled a little. Jake grasped her hipbones, holding on to that hollow place between her hip and leg, and buried his tongue as deep as he could get into her vagina, thrusting in and out while his lower lip pushed and rubbed against her clit.

"Jake..." Mira gasped his name. "Oh God, Jake..." Her thighs quivered. "Oh fuck... Please."

Jake pulled slightly back. "Not yet, love. Soon."

"You're...driving me crazy."

"Good. That's exactly how I want you. Crazy for me and how I make you feel."

She huffed out some jumbled words and Jake smiled.

His response was to spread her cheeks more fully, find her clit again, and suck hard on it and the surrounding tender flesh. He wanted to bury himself inside of her. Feel her come on his face.

And fuck, she did just that. Exploding pleasure mounted all around him as her body jolted and she cried out. Jake lapped at the sudden juiciness of her folds and the quivering aftershocks of her orgasm.

Mira groaned and fell forward on the bed, lying flat on her tummy. Jake, smiling and satisfied, made a deliberate and wet trail with his mouth up her back again toward her neck. He reached for his wallet then and slid out another condom, rolled the thing hurriedly on, and then nudged her legs apart slightly to settle between them. She squirmed and squeaked out a response, mounted her from behind, and slowly eased his now aching and pounding cock into her pussy.

She didn't protest. Of course, he hadn't expected her to.

Jake lowered himself until his face was flush with hers. "I love fucking you, Mira," he whispered. He noticed the rugged rasp to his voice that wasn't there earlier. She affected him in ways he didn't know he could be touched.

He *did* love fucking her. His brain though, kept turning around those words in his head. *I fucking love you, Mira,* his brain said. Love? So soon?

Did he?

Consumed. He was just consumed with her. Right?

Her breathing was even, methodical, and he thrust in and out of her again, echoing the same rhythmic cadence of her slowing pants. She angled her face a little, so her lips aligned with his. She kissed and nibbled at his mouth, their breath mingling.

"Fuck me, Jake Remington," she said, her voice a whisper, perhaps softened by the aftershocks of her powerful orgasm, he thought. She was pliant and willing. There was no way he could not fuck her.

"Take me," she repeated. "Make me yours tonight, Jake."

The words were few and barely whispered but powerful. Jake heard them with this heart, more than with his ears. And he continued to fuck her, his belly flat against her ass, his cock buried deep in her pussy. Their arms both splayed out flat against the bed, his on top of hers with their fingers clasped, and all he wanted was to take her to places she'd never been before.

Perhaps, he was taking himself there, as well.

Fucking Mira was like placing a brand on his heart. His mission had been to claim her, and in turn, she had laid claim to him.

In the process, she had unknowingly ruined him for any other woman. He wondered if she realized that. Likely not. Thing was, he could not imagine another woman to come after her.

The thought was not in the realm of possibility.

I fucking love you, Mira, his brain said again. And he exploded with one of the most powerful orgasms he'd ever experienced.

Mira lay spent underneath Jake, one side of her face flush against the bed, the other with Jake's hot mouth pressed into her temple. He was heavy lying over her, but she didn't care. She loved it. Loved having his body wrapped around her and pinning her tightly to the bed. His breathing was evening out now; earlier, she had felt the rapid-fire cadence of his heart beating hard against her back.

She didn't want him to move. Ever. She wanted to stay like this for a long, long time, his cock deep inside of her and his body protecting her.

It hit her like a lightning bolt that this feeling of protection was something she had craved. Maybe it was the reason why she didn't stay around long with men once she'd been fucked. It was fun getting off, getting them off. She loved getting physical with a man, and the orgasms were a necessary and explosive plus. But that empty feeling that came after always made her leave. No one had ever made her want to stay.

Ever.

Until now. Until Jake.

He stirred and rolled off her, pulling out from between her legs. She groaned and sighed. "No. Please," she said softly, reaching out for him.

Jake didn't go far. He gathered her into him and wrapped his arms around her. She shifted, resting her head on his bicep, her face close to his chest. Jake threw a leg around her hips possessively and drew her even closer into the protective shell of his body.

She was in heaven.

Mira heaved out an immense sigh. She felt encompassed by everything that was Jake. His flesh. His scent. His entire being.

"I love fucking you," Jake whispered into her hair.

Mira didn't say anything for a moment, but squeezed her eyes shut even tighter. Finally, she softly echoed, "I love fucking you back."

Jake groaned and reached between their bodies to unclasp her bra.

"I need every inch of your skin against mine." His voice rasped.

Mira suddenly felt free of everything. Her bra undone, her breasts spilling out between them. She pressed up against Jake's hot chest, desperate to be as close as possible to him.

But Jake wanted something different.

"Mira..."

Her name fell from his lips like a feather-soft breath. Mira tilted her head back to look into his eyes. Jake palmed her left tit and then lowered his face between her breasts. She heard his deep intake of breath followed by a long, healthy sigh.

She clasped his head to her chest and held him there. Jake angled to where he could tongue a nipple. They lay there and he suckled at her softly, teasing her nipple with his teeth, drawing her deeper into his mouth. He stretched to take as much of her inside as he could, and Mira watched his lips move over her.

Moaning, she laid her head back and let Jake play. As his hand moved between her legs, her eyes closed, and she let the sensation roll over her.

Jake moved his fingers in and out of her pussy, teasing her clit much like he was teasing her nipples. He played her body like it was an instrument until she hummed again, on the brink of orgasm. And all she did was lay back and take what he had to offer.

She could get used to this.

Chapter Six

Morning sun slanted sharply across his face. Jake winced, rolled over, and groaned. His bed was empty.

Jerking up to a sitting position, he twisted around to search the room. "Mira!" He shouted her name a little louder than he had intended.

She moved around the corner from the bathroom, wearing only a towel. "Jake?"

He huffed out a breath and his shoulders fell in relief. "Goddamn. I didn't like not knowing where you were."

Mira smiled and rounded the bed. Reaching for his fingers, she sat beside him, placing his hand in her lap and laced her fingers with his. "Jake, I'm here. I wouldn't leave without saying anything."

Again, he heaved out a sigh. "I hope to hell not." Reaching for her with his other hand, he circled her neck and dragged her closer. His lips captured hers and held, leaving her with a wet imprint of his lips on hers. "I can't believe how attached I've gotten to you already," he whispered.

Mira drew back and studied him. She wasn't smiling and that worried him a little. Her eyes searched his, playing back and forth over his face. "I know," she finally said. "I... It's..."

"Different."

She nodded, and then finally gave him a shy smile. "Yes."

He fiddled with the towel at her breasts. Her skin was damp, he noticed, as he tucked his forefinger inside her cleavage. The dewy softness of her skin there excited him. "You took a shower." His cock thickened, wishing he'd known. He would have loved to join her there.

Her head dipped again. "Yes. I have to go to work, Jake. Soon."

She fiddled with his fingers, still in her lap.

"Ah, hell. I was hoping for a few more hours." He paused, stroking her hair. "What time are you finished today?"

"I'm already an hour late. I called in to start at seven, end at three."

"Then I'll meet you back here at three," he said.

Mira shook her head. "No, Jake. I need to go home. I have things to do there. I'm sure my father is worried about me. I need to call him since I didn't come in last night."

"Your father?"

"Yes. I live with him."

"Then hell, I guess he's worried. Did you call him?"

"No, I will in a few minutes. I left my purse in your truck with my cell phone."

"I'll go get it. You need to let him know." Jake stood and reached for his jeans, pulling them over his body, sans underwear. Then he stopped and faced her. "I really want to see you again this afternoon, Mira. As soon as possible."

She stared at him. "Jake, I... I can't see you while I'm working. Chandler West would have my neck. And my father depends on me for certain things, so I have to go home. You understand that, right?"

He nodded. "Of course. Family comes first. Always. And I realize Chandler runs a tight ship, but you don't have to worry about me, Mira. I'm not going to do anything to jeopardize your job."

Jake watched her shoulders relax.

"Good," she said. "Because I need this job."

For a moment, Jake studied her. He had to wonder exactly why a woman like Mira was working as a housekeeper in a hotel, anyway. Of course, that was none of his business—but she just didn't seem the type. As if a housekeeper had a type....

"I need to get ready." Mira turned and headed back for the bathroom.

"I'd still like to meet you back here at three."

She faced him. "In the lobby."

He conceded. "All right. And I will take you home. After all, I'm the reason you didn't get home. Perhaps I can meet your father."

The look she gave him then was one of near fear. She froze, staring at him.

"Mira?"

"Oh, sure." She finally said. "Why don't you run down and get my purse. I'll finish up here and will be waiting for you."

He agreed, a little concerned that perhaps she might not be there when he returned. But she needed her purse and cell phone, right? "I'll be right back," he told her, pulling on a T-shirt.

"Okay."

Taking a few steps toward her, he kissed her gently on the lips. "It's all good, Mira," he said softly. "No worries, all right?"

But her face was the epitome of worry. He didn't know why, but he intended to find out.

Mira watched Jake leave and then sat on the edge of the bed with a sigh. Closing her eyes, she inhaled deep—an attempt to rid herself of the butterflies in her tummy. This night—and Jake—had left her with an incredible sense of peace, mixed with scary-as-shit emotions that she couldn't quite put her finger on.

She felt good with him. She liked him a whole helluva lot. But he was a Remington, and she was the daughter of a recovering alcoholic, ex-bronc-riding, ranch hand who lived an entirely different lifestyle from the man she spent the past several hours with.

There is no future here. Her future likely was with some cowboy somewhere who wanted to settle down with a wife and kids on a small ranch of his own one day. And there was nothing wrong with that.

Nothing at all. Except Mira wasn't the kind of girl to settle for ordinary—even though ordinary was what she grew up with.

Hell, she *could* settle for ordinary if it were the right guy and he was good to her. She knew she could. And Poppy kept dropping hints that she needed to find that guy and give him grandchildren before he died. But she was only twenty-five and she wasn't ready for kids. Hells bells. She could barely take care of herself.

Frowning, she glanced off. No. That wasn't true. She'd been taking care of herself for a long time and she'd done just fine. Taking care of her mom before she died, her little brother too, who was safe—away at college—and now her dad. Yeah, she was good at taking care of others. But what about herself? Maybe that was the thing—maybe she wasn't so good at making sure her own needs were met. Maybe. Maybe that's why she went a little wild with sex sometimes.

She just wanted to feel and lay back and enjoy. Let somebody else take the reins for a while.

Maybe she secretly wanted someone to take care of her. As independent as she was, that sounded sort of good, even if she didn't want to admit it.

But Jake Remington? No. It would never work. Socially, they weren't even close to being on the same playing field.

She laughed. Jake Remington was all wrong for her.

She rose from the bed and paced back and forth. Nervous. Where in the hell was he though? She needed to call. Needed to get to work.

Needed to get out of this room as soon as possible before anyone saw her leave. She always kept a spare uniform in her locker so she could change quickly in the restroom downstairs. She had no choice but to wear the red dress to the lobby though. Hopefully, she could side-step anyone who might want to point out the fact that her barhopping dress wasn't exactly appropriate lodge attire. She looked more like a hooker than a guest.

No matter.

She glanced at the digital clock on the bedside table. Twelve minutes until she had to clock in. Drumming her fingers on the armoire, she glanced toward the window, then crossed the room to look out over the parking lot.

Her heart stopped. Jake stood by his truck talking to Chandler.

"No. No, no, no, no. *No!*"

As fast as she could manage, she slipped into her dress and shoes, out Jake's hotel room door, and headed toward the stairwell, praying it was empty.

It was.

Thank God. She changed her clothes and clocked in to work with two minutes to spare. During that transition, she tried like hell to push Jake out of her head—and her heart.

It wasn't easy. But she tried. She had work to do.

Three hours and six cleaned rooms later, Mira ducked out of room 301 to grab some toiletries off her cart and ran head-on into her boss.

"Oh!"

"Slow down there, Mira." Chandler steadied her by grasping her forearms. "Where's the fire?"

She shook herself. "No fire. Just trying to get my work done, sir."

Chandler scowled. "Cut the *sir* bullshit, Mira. I've known you since you were a kid."

Mira tilted her chin. "I realize that Chandler. I'm just trying to be professional. That is something you have asked of me. Right? Professionalism?"

He crossed his arms and ignored her sarcastic comeback. After a moment, he asked, "How's your Pop?"

She shrugged. "He's okay. Bored. He's ready to get back to work. Mentally anyway. Physically, not so much. He thinks he's in way better shape than he is."

"You know I feel terrible about this and all."

Mira nodded her acknowledgement. "I know that Chandler. And so does he. We're just grateful that he'll still have a job when he's well. Thank you for that."

"I wouldn't have it any other way."

"I know. You're a good man. Even if…" She clamped her mouth shut tight. Why did she have to say that?

But Chandler grinned. "Even if I give you hell because you're a loose woman?"

"Shit, Chandler." She turned and shoved some tiny shampoo and conditioner bottles into her dress pockets. "You don't have to put it that way. I just…"

"Like men. I know."

She turned and pointed a finger at his chest. "And before you got married, you were quite the rounder yourself, I might add. Or so I've heard."

"Indeed. But not in my place of business. You damn well know how I feel about that. I can't have the lodge prostituted in that way."

That statement riled Mira to no end. "Prostituted! Hells bells, Chandler!" Her voice raised. "I'm not some low-life whore! And I'm definitely not a prostitute!" She shoved another handful of shampoo into her pocket and whirled toward the hotel room door.

Chandler grabbed her elbow. "Now hold your horses. That's not what I said."

She spun back. "Well that's what I heard. I am not like that and don't you fucking dare put that kind of label on me!" She jerked out of his grasp and headed into the bathroom, tiny bottles falling to the floor.

"Dammit, Mira." Chandler followed her. "Let me rephrase. I don't want this place perceived as being a place where you can pick up an easy piece of ass for the asking. You get that, don't you?"

She placed the shampoo in its place on the counter, and then looked at him through the mirror. "It was one time, Chandler. Once. I told you I wouldn't do it again and I haven't."

Well, shit. That's not true. Now. But Jake is different.

"I believe it was twice."

She glared. "Only if you count the parking lot."

"I do."

"Shit, Chandler. Leave me alone. I told you I wouldn't do it again and I won't." She pushed past him and out the hotel room door, reaching for her dust cloth on the cart. She looked up to see Jake standing on the other side of the cart with her purse in his hand.

How long had he been standing there and what had he heard?

"Mira?"

She started to shake her head, hoping he would be quiet, when Chandler followed her out into the hallway. "All right, Mira. Whatever you say," Chandler said. Then looking away from her, he added, "Remington?"

Mira stared at her purse and knit her brows, trying to give Jake a signal to hide the damn thing. She turned toward Chandler. "He's looking for his room. I think he's on the wrong floor." She glared back at Jake again.

Jake put her purse behind his back and nodded. "Yeah. Damnedest thing. I guess I got off on three rather than two. My bad."

"Happens all the time," Chandler said, edging around the cart. "While you're here though, if you have a minute, let's continue that business discussion we started in the parking lot this morning."

Jake nodded, looking straight at Chandler, and avoiding her. Good. He turned away and started walking with Chandler down the hallway, then turned back. "Oh honey," he said. "I found this in the elevator. Can you turn it into lost and found for me?" He laid her purse on the cart with a wink. Mira didn't react but reached for the bag.

"Of course, sir. I'm happy to do so."

He grinned. "Thanks." Then he turned back and met up with Chandler.

Shit. She was in trouble. *What the fuck kind of business did Jake Remington have with Chandler West?*

Jake listened to every word Chandler said but heard little of his speech. His focus was back on Mira and the snippet of conversation he'd heard while he stood in the hallway. She and Chandler sure weren't talking like they had an employer-employee relationship. Sounded like more to it than that.

"So, I'll have to get back to you on those details, Remington, but would you please call off the wolves and tell them I have things under control? Remington?"

Jake shook himself and looked at Chandler. "Say that again?"

Chandler stood behind his desk. They were seated in Chandler's office behind the main desk off the lobby. "You didn't hear a damn word I said."

Jake exhaled. "Sure, I did. Your men found the squatters on the back eighty acres that connects with my parents' ranch and the Hargrove land. You'll take care of it."

Hands on his hips, Chandler stared at Jake. "You got enough to spit back few things, but I guess that's enough for now. Yes, I'll take care of it even though it's not all my problem. Just make sure the Hargroves and your parents know I'll handle it. With your folks in Florida and old man Hargrove three feet from the grave, I'll do the neighborly thing."

"So, it's not your people building over the line then?"

"No. Likely some squatters trying to take advantage of some antiquated boundary laws—but believe you me, I don't want them there any more than anyone else. I'll send Brice and some boys over there tomorrow. I guarantee you they will move on."

Jake nodded. "All right, then. I guess my work here is done."

He stood.

Chandler added, "Now, tell me what's going on between you and Mira."

Stunned at the question, Jake pinned his gaze on Chandler's face. "I don't know what you are talking about."

Chandler looked to the floor and slowly shook his head. "Now, I'm an observant man, Jake. I don't have any proof, of course, but the eye contact between the two of you a few minutes ago said a whole lot more than *I'm on the wrong floor.*"

"Well, you observed wrong." Jake headed for the door, twisted the doorknob, and opened it. He stepped partially out into the lobby.

"You're sure about that? Because I'm warning you to keep your hands off her, Remington. You're not good enough for my goddaughter."

Jake turned back. "Your goddaughter?"

"Yes."

"I had no idea."

"Obviously. But that act in the hallway didn't fool me. Did you sleep with her last night? Did she stay with you in your hotel room? Because if she did, goddaughter or not, I will fire her ass..."

Jake interrupted him. "Hell no, Chandler! I told you, those days are gone. I don't fuck and run anymore."

Chandler crossed the room. "Look, Remington. Everyone around here knows your reputation. You fuck and run every time you get a chance, even if it gets you or someone else into trouble."

"Not this time." Jake glared at Chandler. *I am not running away from Mira.* "Besides," he added, "your goddaughter is definitely not my type. A little chunky to my liking and she's a damn hotel maid, for crap's sake. Don't get me wrong, seeing that she's practically family and all, but I don't date hotel maids."

"You just fuck them?"

Jake narrowed his gaze. "That's between me and the maid."

He paused, watching Chandler's gaze drift off behind his right shoulder.

Jake turned to see Mira standing no more than five feet behind him. The look on her face told him everything he needed to know. She'd heard his harsh words and was obviously horrified at what he said.

Shit. Shit!

Without blinking an eye, Mira turned and ran away. Jake just stood there and watched her go.

Chandler swore behind him. "Hell, Remington. Now I gotta go fire that girl. And you?"

Jake turned back. "What?"

"You get out of my sight and don't you ever come near her again. You got me?"

Swallowing hard, Jake dipped his head in a nod. "I got you."

Chapter Seven

Mira ran blindly through the hotel lobby and down the long hallway that led out the back of the hotel. She pushed through the door and burst into the parking lot, suddenly remembering she had no vehicle and no way to get home.

Dammit, her pick-up was still at Tory's.

She needed out of there, and fast. No way was she going to stick around for a scene with Chandler. Or with Jake, for that matter. She needed to go.

Frantic, her gaze skittered about. The only people who parked in back lot were staff, and obviously, they were all working. Plenty of cars. No freaking people. She stood in the parking lot alone.

Dammit. She needed to go and *now.* "Where is everyone?"

All at once, her eyelids stung, and tears rushed down her face. She sobbed, sucked in a ragged breath, fisted her hands, and stomped her feet. "Dammit!"

But a tantrum right there in the parking lot was not going to do her a damn bit of good. She needed to get a grip. Covering her face, she sat on the curb, feeling a bit defeated. A few seconds later, she uncovered her eyes to see a pickup truck rounding the corner of the hotel and parking abruptly in front of her, screeching tires, and all. The window slowly rolled down.

She swiped at her eyes and looked at Jake staring back at her.

"Mira, it's not what you think. Please, just get in the truck. Okay? Let's talk."

She glanced away. "I don't want to talk to you, Jake Remington."

"I know you don't," he said, "but you need to talk to me. C'mon Mira. I'll take you home."

"I'll find my own fucking ride home."

"You already have one. I'm right here, right now."

She stood, her fists perched on each hip. "If you think for one minute I'm getting in that truck with you, then you have another think coming. I'm not." She could be stubborn as an old damn mule when she wanted to be.

Jake switched off the truck and threw open the door. He got out, took a couple of steps, and stood before her, his feet spread wide. Blowing out a quick breath, he said, "Mira, look. We need to talk. What you heard—"

"What I heard is all I need to hear. Now go. I don't want to see you or go anywhere with you. Ever." She tilted her chin. "I don't need it spelled out to me that I'm beneath you."

"Ah, shit. You know that's not true."

"I don't know anything. I'm just a lowly maid, and a chunky one at that."

"Stop it."

"Just go, Jake. I'm not leaving here with you."

He studied her. "All right." Jake crossed his arms over his chest. "Then I guess we are at a stand-off. I'm not going anywhere until you agree to talk with me. And it looks like you're not budging either, so here we are."

Mira crossed her arms too, mirroring his stance. Except, she tapped the toe of her shoe on the hard pavement. Antsy. She was too antsy. She couldn't stand here like this for long without blasting him and telling him *exactly* what she thought.

And she really and truly didn't want to do that, because she wasn't entirely sure what she *had* heard. Maybe she'd misunderstood? No. He'd dissed her big time.

The maid.

Fucker.

She glared at him. They stood that way for what seemed a small eternity. Finally, she threw up her hands and stomped off around the tailgate of the truck. "Get in the goddamned truck, Jake. Do it before I change my fucking mind!"

She ignored the slight smile she saw crack across his face as she pulled open the passenger side door. "Fucking the chunky maid my foot," she whispered to herself.

Jake cleared his throat and shut the driver's side door. Looking straight at Mira, he said, "You have a bit of a potty mouth."

"I do when I'm angry." She stared straight ahead. "So, get used to it."

Inwardly, Jake smiled. "So that means you're not ditching me for some rude and crude Neanderthal cowboy?"

"No. It doesn't mean that. It means... Hell. Just drive."

"I will. Calm down, Mira. We're going to work this out."

She twisted to look at him. "Don't fucking tell me to calm down, Jake Remington. No one tells me to fucking calm down."

Jake took a deep breath and started the truck. "Sorry. Look. I'm trying to make amends here."

"Well, you have a funny way of doing that."

"Obviously. Let's just not talk for a few minutes and think this through before speaking. I think that's my only defense at this point."

He accelerated and rounded the back of the hotel. Out of the corner of his eye, he watched Mira sit back and look out the passenger side window. "Damned straight," she said.

Jake smiled again and drove toward the main road. He stopped before pulling out onto the highway. "Right or left?"

Mira didn't blink an eye. "Left. And stop smiling."

He tried like hell to do that, but it was difficult. She was softening and that was a good thing. "All right." He turned left and drove for several miles before either of them broke the silence.

"You'll have to tell me where to go," he told her.

She looked at him. "Hell? Hm. Somehow I figured you already knew the directions there."

"Very funny, Mira."

"I'm not laughing."

He took a deep breath. "Neither am I because none of this is funny."

"That's right, it isn't."

"So, you're Chandler West's goddaughter?"

She shrugged. "He calls me that. He knew my dad back in their rodeo days. I barely remember him when I was a kid. There's nothing special there between us and the goddaughter thing doesn't mean anything, really. I don't even go to church so I'm not entirely sure what that means." She glanced off, out the window. "He's my boss. That's about it."

"I see. Usually someone who steps up to take care of you at baptism is a big deal. You're sure you aren't more to him than that?"

"Humpht."

"I don't know what that means."

She glanced his way. "That means that I know him. I've...well, I've known him all my life. That's it."

The truck cab fell silent for a while. He had to wonder what that meant—that Mira's dad and Chandler somehow had connections. Probably rodeo. Or the ranch. Sounded like there was more to the story but he wasn't about to touch that unless she opened the door a little farther.

They rode for several more miles without talking. Jake hoped to hell she was leading him in the right direction. On all counts.

"So you're close with the Wests, then," he queried, wondering if it was crossing the line.

"Not really."

"Doesn't sound like that to me."

She looked back. "My dad worked for the Wests, okay? No big deal. We're hired help. Nothing special."

Jake cringed at that. "I don't know why you put yourself down so much, Mira. I think you're pretty damn special."

"Right." She laughed. "Fuck the chunky maid special, huh?"

Jake braked in the middle of the road and threw the gearshift into park. He turned to face her directly. Her denigrating herself really pissed him off. He sure wished she wouldn't do that. "Look, Mira. Honey... I didn't want to get into this while driving, but..."

"But you did when you started asking questions, Jake. Believe me, I wouldn't have gone there."

He reached for a tendril of her hair. "I loved fucking you Mira. That wasn't a lie."

"So, you like fucking the chunky maid type after all, huh?"

"Would you stop it? I like fucking *you*. I love your curves. Your rosy plump lips. How your hips fit into my hands. How your breasts feel when I..."

Sighing, he dropped the curl and added, "I care about you, Mira. I know it's only been hours, but I do. And yes, I lied. I didn't want to let on to Chandler that I'd been with you. I heard loud and clear earlier in the night that you didn't want anyone to know you were with me."

"Or rather, that I was with you in your room."

"I get that."

"You could have just said no to him. You didn't have to over-exaggerate with the chunky maid shit. That was insulting." She sat a little straighter and taller in her seat. "I mean, I am the way I am. I like my curves. And I've not always been a maid, you know. I just..."

She clamped her mouth shut.

"You just what?"

"Nothing." She faced ahead. "Let's go. Turn left right up there." She pointed.

Jake didn't move. She shot a look his way. "Let's *go*."

"In a minute." He tucked a finger under her chin. "Mira, look at me and listen to what I'm about to say. I didn't want you to get into trouble, so I lied and yes, I over did it. But make no mistake about it, honey. I love your curves. All of them."

His gaze dropped to her open-collared dress and the cleavage beyond. "In fact, I adore every delicious inch..." He leaned in and was tempted to take a lick but thought better of it. He pulled back.

Jake watched Mira's mouth twitch, as if she wanted to smile but wouldn't let herself.

"I'm *not* chunky," she said.

"No, you're not. You're beautiful."

"But I *am* a maid."

"That's not a problem."

"You hire maids."

"I just said that. It didn't mean a damn thing."

"I wasn't always a maid. I used to be a journalist. I'm a writer."

"See? That wasn't so difficult, was it?"

"What?"

"Talking about yourself."

Mira sighed. "You seem to bring things out in me."

Jake smiled and lowered his voice. "I'd like to hear more about that." A horn sounded abruptly down the road behind them. Jake glanced into the rearview mirror and put the truck back into drive. "But later. So, we turn left up here?"

"Yeah."

As they drew closer to the ranch gate where he was supposed to turn left, Jake grew more puzzled. "You live at West Hills Ranch?" Jake turned off the main highway onto the ranch road.

"Not at the main house, of course." Mira sucked in a breath and exhaled long. "We'll turn before you get there. We're ranch hands, like I told you. My daddy works for the Wests. Or worked. Right now, he's not doing much of anything. Turn there."

Jake did. He'd not traveled this road before, even with all the times he'd been on the West's Ranch. The dirt road curved wide around the main house and buildings and headed toward the hillier part of the ranch. He glanced sideways at Mira. "I want you to know, just in case there is some crazy notion rolling around in your head, that I don't care one iota about you being a hotel maid or that your father was a ranch hand. Hard work is respectable, no matter what it is."

Mira cocked her head to the side and smiled. "So, what you are trying to tell me, Jake Remington, is that I'm good enough for you?"

He nodded. "Yes. I am definitely saying that." Then he frowned. "Thing is, Chandler was probably right. It's entirely likely that I am not good enough for you."

The look on Mira's face surprised him. "I don't understand," she whispered.

He looked ahead and parked the truck, ignoring her statement and the fact that he'd brought up a subject he didn't want to explore any further. "This must be your house?"

Mira nodded, looking out the windshield. "Yes. And there is my Poppy sitting on the porch." Her hand went to the door latch. "I better go. Thanks for the ride."

"Wait." Jake touched her arm. "Mira, with your permission, I'd like to meet your dad. And I'd like to stay for a while so that we can talk more later. May I?"

He watched her chest rise and fall with her even breaths while she studied his face. Finally, she said, "All right, Jake. All right. Come meet my Pop."

Mira smiled at her father as she neared the porch. She climbed the three rickety steps and crossed the rough wooden floor to where he sat in an old rocker. She leaned in and gave him a kiss on the cheek. "Hi Poppy," she said. "I'm home early."

He smirked and nodded. "Chandler called. Said you flew out of there a few hours early and wondered if you were okay. Said you were to call him when I saw you."

Mira straightened. "All right. I'll give him a call."

Her Poppy narrowed his gaze. "You okay girl? I worried about you all night."

"I called you as soon as I could, Pop. I told you that this morning. I was with the girls and we stayed out too late. My phone went dead."

Her father harrumphed then cocked his head toward Jake. "Who's this?"

"Ah, Poppy. This is Jake. He offered me a ride home. He was..."

Jake stepped forward. "Nice to meet you, sir. I had some business with the West's and told Mira I would be happy to drop her off."

Mira watched her father eyeball Jake's hand and then finally shake it. "Name?"

"I'm Jake Remington, sir."

Mira's dad tipped his head back. "Ah. Now I know the reason for the smooth hand. No calluses. You're not a rancher."

Jake shook his head. "No, sir. I'm a lawyer. I have a practice in Kentucky, although the farm I run up there takes up a lot of my time these days."

Mira sucked in a sharp breath. Lawyer? *Shit.*

"Farm?" Her father spit out. "Down here we call them ranches."

"That we do," Jake told him quickly. "Ranch, farm, makes no difference. The work is hard either way you look at it and everything is a gamble."

Her Pop cocked an eyebrow. "How so?"

"Animals and people—they are both unpredictable," he said, leaning a little closer toward her father.

Mira thought she should intervene. "Jake is from around here, Pop. Quit giving him the third degree."

"I know that," he said, his gaze hooked with Jake's. "You're *that* Remington," he added then. "I remember. Left out of here, what? Six years or so ago? I read the papers."

Mira watched Jake's face turn a little pale—but then he squared his shoulders and stood a little taller. "Yes, sir. I did leave about six years ago. My parents still live on the ranch and I'm here visiting for a few days. Had some business in the area."

Her Pop gave Jake a narrow-eyed glare. "That right. Well keep your business up the road there, son. And keep your damn hands off my little girl. You hear me?"

Mira's chest exploded. "Poppy! That was uncalled for." She turned to Jake. "I'm sorry. He's on medication and..."

Her father rose slowly, pushing up to a standing position by anchoring his hands on the chair arms. "That has nothing to damn do with it, Mira. I might not have my legs, but I still have my brain. This man is bad news. You stay the hell away from him."

Her heart cracked. She looked toward Jake, who just stood there with his eyes locked on her father. Finally, after a long silent moment, he turned to Mira and said. "He's right. Listen to your Pop, Mira. I'm bad news and I'll be on my way."

He turned on his heel and left. Mira didn't move. She simply watched him walk out of her life.

Chapter Eight

An hour later, Mira shoved the casserole in the oven and turned to face her father. He sat at the kitchen table—an old wooden dinette set he and her mother had bought when they married—and drummed his fingers on the Formica top.

She turned to face him. "I have never been so humiliated in my life," she told him. "What gives you the right to dictate who I see and what I do? I'm a grown woman."

"And I'm still your old man."

"An old man who drinks too much and has no filters. You say whatever is on your damn mind, no matter who you hurt."

"Hurt? Who did I hurt, Mira? You?"

"Yes!"

"Hell. I saved you from hurt."

Mira bristled. "Is that what you call it?" Her voice rose. Suddenly years of his blunt, narrow-minded attitude welled up inside her. And it had nothing to do with saving anyone from hurt. "Is that what you called it all of the times you were so brutally honest with mom and with my brother and me all our lives? Saving us from hurt?" She laughed and threw her hands up in the air. "You have no idea what you did to any of us, do you?"

Her father stood, the chair screeching on the floor underneath him. "I don't believe in sugar-coating anything, darlin'. You know that. The truth is at least straightforward and direct. I say things how I see 'em. And you and your mother and that bastard brother of yours deserved the truth."

Bastard brother. Mira cringed at the words. She'd hated when her Pop had called her brother that. "Honesty isn't always the best policy. Bobby loved you until you had to go and be so damned honest."

"He needed to know he wasn't my kid."

"And you broke his heart when you did it. Don't you get it Pop? Sometimes the truth doesn't need to be so damn brutal."

"This ain't about Bobby, girl. It's about you. You need to know the kind of man that Remington is. No good. Just go read the papers from about six years ago. It's all there for public knowledge. So yeah, I said what I thought, and I meant what I said. He better stay the hell away. That man would give you nothing but a lifetime of hurt."

"Shit, Pop. I only just met him. I wasn't going to marry him, for cripe's sake. I've barely known him twenty-four hours."

"According to Chandler, you know him pretty intimately for only knowing him twenty-four hours."

"Chandler West doesn't know shit. Besides, what I do is none of his damn business. He's full of crap."

"Wouldn't be the first time you got caught with your legs in the air. I wouldn't expect anything less from you this time. Especially dressed like you were last night."

Mira exhaled sharply. "I was out with the girls."

"So, you didn't get fucked? That dress was screaming 'fuck me' darlin'"

"That's none of your damn business," she fired back.

"It *is* my business if you lose your job."

"Why? Because then there's no one to put food on the table? Is that it Poppy? After all, you have to save whatever meager bit of money you get from the West's for beer and whatever the hell painkiller it is you score from the streets."

Her father cleared his throat. "Chandler's going to fire you."

"Then I'll find another job."

"Tried that once, didn't you? How'd that work out for you? Hell, girl, you're never going to amount to much more than a hotel maid, anyway. Maybe you could handle being a waitress but I dunno. You need to have some people skills for that. Something other than shaking that ass of yours."

Frustrated, Mira turned back to the stove, clenching and unclenching her fists. Every argument she'd overheard of her parents for years welled upside her with the same kind of hurt. Her gut literally trembled with not only the anguish and sting from the words cutting into her right now, but for the pain he had inflicted on all of them her entire life. Her mother internalized it all until it made her sick. Well, Mira wasn't going to let him do the same thing to her. She didn't want to argue but he could be so damn aggravating. Especially when he was drinking. She learned over the stove and spoke to the wall. "You know nothing about me, what I can do or want to do, or anything. You have no idea of my talents or my dreams or who I want to be as a woman, Poppy. I'm sorry to say that but it's true. Somehow, you managed to miss a big part of my life when you were out drinking and running around on Mom."

She heard him step up behind her, but she didn't glance back.

"Now you look here, girl," he growled. "Whatever happened between me and your mom—that was between us. Had nothing to do with you."

Whirling back, she lashed out. "It sure as hell *did* have something to do with me, Pop. It had *everything* to do with me! Every damn time you stepped out on Mom, argued with her, and yelled at her until she was in tears, I was the one left behind to pick up the pieces. Me, Pop. *Me!* I'm the one who was here for her when you were nowhere to be found and her heart was breaking."

"Never asked you to pick up the pieces, girl."

She shook her finger at him. "No. No, you didn't. But I did anyway. Now, you look here, Pop. I chose to stay behind and pick up the goddamned pieces because I loved her! Something you wouldn't know anything thing about. But now that Mom's gone, and Bobby's probably never coming back here again, I'm done. For some reason I kept thinking I needed to stay around here and keep your damn ass alive, but I don't know what in the hell I was thinking. You don't give a shit whether you live or die and I'm not sticking around to let you ruin my life, too."

He cleared his throat. "Mira…"

But she was not going to let him interrupt her. "All I've done for years is take care of people. Mom, Bobby, and now you all the damn time. I'm sorry that horse threw you and busted your back and legs but guess what? If you hadn't been drunk, it wouldn't have happened. Not my fault. So just for the record, I'm tired of being your housemaid, cook, and chief bottle washer. I'm tired of working two jobs just to keep groceries on the table for you. Especially when you don't even appreciate it. I'm more than a damn maid. I want more out of my life. I'm *good enough* to do anything in life I want to do. But if you can't see that…and if that's all I am to you, then I'm truly and forever done."

"You ain't done girl. You need me whether you think you do or not."

Mira stood her ground. "Now that's where you're wrong, Pop. I can make my own way in the world. It's time I move out anyway and get started on that plan. I've put it off long enough."

"And what plan is that?"

She squared her shoulders. "Finishing school. Getting my degree."

Her Pop snorted. "Damn degree. Money you don't need to spend. You just need to work harder, Mira. You don't need no damn degree to get you where you're going in life."

She stood her ground. "Actually, I do, Pop. There's a job downtown I want. And it may take a couple of more years of school before I can get it, but *I will get it*." She turned and set the timer on the stove. "Now, I'm going to go pack. This casserole will be ready in twenty minutes."

"Pack? Now where you gonna go, girl?"

She turned. "I'll figure that out. I have friends. I'll get an apartment."

"Then you best rely on those friends, 'cause you're not getting anything from me."

She shook her head. "Don't worry about that, Pop. I won't ask you for one damn red cent." She headed down the hallway.

Her father shuffled after her. "You leave here girl? Just remember this. You don't come back."

Mira stopped and stood, the dinette table between them now, and gave him a long stare. "If that's the way you want it."

"It is."

"Then we're in agreement."

He nodded. "Don't come crawlin' back, girl, because I won't take you," he repeated.

Mira cocked her head to the side. "You don't have to tell me twice."

Jake tossed his luggage on the bed and watched the dust bunnies dance in the sun-streak angling away from the window. He had checked out of the lodge a couple of hours earlier and headed to his parents' ranch—the home he grew up in. He knew right where the key was hidden on the porch and hadn't been worried in the least if it wasn't there. He'd broken into his house many a time in his youth when he'd gotten home after curfew.

Today was different, though. He'd called his parents and told them he'd like to stay a couple of days at the ranch and they'd asked if he could oversee the last of the remodeling that was happening in the kitchen. He'd told them he'd be happy to do so. Truth be told, he was glad to have something to do. It gave him purpose. A reason to hang around.

Not that he shouldn't be getting back to Kentucky. He should, and soon. There was business waiting there as well but he could handle most of it from afar. His private law practice was his mainstay with the horse farm a growing supplemental income. He'd always loved horses, and this was a different kind of horse ranching, you might say, but it was familiar all the same.

Setting a short tumbler of bourbon and ice he'd mixed for himself downstairs on the cherry dresser top, he pulled a pint of one of Kentucky's finest bourbons out of his pocket and set it next to the glass. Shrugging out of his jacket, he tossed it over a straight back chair next to the window. Simultaneously kicking out of his boots, he let them lay where they fell on the floor. After a hefty swig of the bourbon—which emptied the glass—he poured another shot or so over the ice.

He sighed and then sat on the edge of the bed, his head full of things he should and shouldn't be thinking. He was troubled, uneasy, and a little out-of-sorts. While he knew why, he didn't want to admit it to himself.

Ranches not farms. Of course, like what Mira's father had said, in Kentucky they were called farms, not ranches. And the horses were thoroughbreds, not quarter horses. Not to mention, two entirely different cultures of horse people.

He'd gotten sucked into the thoroughbred horse industry when he was in college at the University of Louisville. November and May were his two favorite months, when the horses were running at Churchill Downs. And if he couldn't wait for those months, he'd head to Lexington in April and October for the races there at Keeneland. He'd learned that if one can't come to respect and admire the tradition, pomp, and circumstance of thoroughbred horseracing, and in particular the Kentucky Derby, one would have a difficult time existing within the culture of the city of Louisville. Horses—not to mention bourbon—were a way of life. And before long, Jake had made both his.

This trip back to Texas though had made him a tad homesick for his old Texas lifestyle and he pondered how he could bring a little Texas back with him to Kentucky.

That thought intrigued him.

Mira? Would that bit of Texas keep him happy and satisfied in Kentucky?

No. He huffed out a breath and sat on the edge of the bed, tenting his hands with his fingers. Mira wasn't a piece of chattel to be acquired and owned. Not a decision to be made just because he was feeling a little melancholy. No. Besides, she had some say-so in that too and likely right now, she wasn't too high on him—walking out on her like he did.

He'd be better off investing in a small herd of longhorns to take north.

Yes. Maybe that was it. Longhorns in Kentucky would be an oddity, but he liked the sound of it. A lot. He rose and made a note in his cell phone. If he had time, he'd swing by a few ranches he knew of in the area and see about a couple of bulls and a cow or two.

Like he didn't have enough to do—but he wasn't the kind of person to settle on one thing. Practicing law was his profession. Ranching, farming, was his life. His passion.

After his law practice was established, he'd bought the original small farm outside of Lexington. He lucked upon some land on the edge of Bluegrass horse country and over time, bought some of the smaller farms surrounding it and added to his domain. In time, he'd acquired a patchwork of paddocks with black fences, majestic horse barns, manicured lawns and fields, and a southern-style Antebellum mansion he now called home.

He *should* be getting back there—his business here with the West's was finished. But something was keeping him from going. He just couldn't go...not yet anyway.

He'd left things undone with Mira. Just walked out. No sense of closure.

But is that what he wanted? Closure?

He didn't. No way in hell he wanted to close this short chapter of his life with her. Right now, he just needed time to think. Mira Featherstone had jerked a knot in his life and he needed to figure out how to untangle this mess.

He *should* be getting back home. He *shouldn't* be thinking so damn much about Mira. Had he screwed up back at her house when he'd abruptly and rudely walked out of her life? Probably. But her father had hit a nerve, and even though he'd been thinking along those same lines—that he wasn't good enough for Mira—hearing her father voice it made him turn tail and run.

And that wasn't like him. He wasn't the kind of man who ducked responsibility or obligation. Not that Mira was either one of those things. Mira was what he wanted, plain and simple, and he wasn't ready to give her up. Yet, he'd let the words of an old man get to him. But he wasn't just any old man, he was her father. And that mattered, didn't it?

The sins of his past had literally come back to haunt him in a way he had never imagined. It took her father smacking him upside the head with reality to make him see.

It didn't matter how successful he was back in Kentucky. He'd always be the rich rancher kid with the bad reputation with women.

But what could he do about that?

Nothing now. His head was too fuzzy with the bourbon and he needed sleep. He'd figure it all out tomorrow.

He glanced about. He'd not been in this room for several years. His old room. Perusing the space, he noticed his mother still hadn't moved his rodeo buckles and his football trophies. He laughed out loud thinking that all those trophies should amount to something. Shouldn't they? He'd not *always* been bad news.

His high school senior picture still sat on his dresser. He imagined when he looked in the closet, he'd still find his high school wardrobe—particularly his letter jacket—hanging there.

Later. He'd look later. *Right now, all I want is sleep.*

Retrieving both the glass and the bottle, he set them on the nightstand by the bed, throwing back another hefty drink before he did so. Then stripping the covers and sheets back, he dropped his bag to the floor. He sat on the bed and laid back. Splitting damn headache. Maybe he should switch to coffee.

No. What he needed was more bourbon and sleep. All he wanted was to be comatose so maybe then, just maybe, he could get the hurt look on Mira's face out of his head.

"I can put you up in 201 for the night if you want. Then tomorrow you can start looking for a place to live."

Mira closed her eyes to shut Madeleine's face out of her line of vision. Behind her eyelids, she saw Jake lying in the bed in 201. She lay there next to him while he suckled at her breasts and toyed with her clit. "Isn't there another room besides 201?" She opened her eyes again to look at her friend.

Madeleine shook her head. "All booked up. They guy in 201 checked out late today but there are no late check-ins scheduled for tonight, so it is open. But I have to tell you, Mira, it won't be open after tonight. We're heating up for the season."

She knew that. Summer was upon them. But she wasn't worried about that. She was more worried about something else.

"So, he checked out?"

"Who?"

"The guy in 201 with the caiman boots."

"Yes. A couple of hours ago, like I said."

Mira's thoughts drifted. A couple of hours ago wouldn't have been long after he'd left her place. It sure didn't take Jake long to get the hell out of there. But could she blame him? Her father had been rude. But a part of her had wanted him to stand up to her Pop and put him in his place.

But of course, he hadn't. And why should he?

Jake wasn't anything to her. Not really. Another one-night stand. Right?

"Mira?"

She looked at Madeleine and didn't really see her at all. "All right. I'll take it. I'm not on the schedule for tomorrow so I'll start looking for an apartment first thing in the morning." She lifted her bag onto her shoulder and glanced about. "But I suppose I should start looking for a job too. I guess I don't still have this one, do I?"

Madeleine shrugged. "I don't know, honey. Chandler never said anything to me, but he doesn't share that kind of stuff with me. Maybe it's best though you just find something in town. That way you can separate yourself from the Wests all the way around. You're sure you want to move out from home, honey?"

Mira peered at Madeleine. "Yes. It's a long story and maybe I'll tell you one day but moving out is in my best interest." She paused and glanced behind the counter. "Is that today's paper? I heard they were hiring down in Kerrville, you know, at some of those big box stores. Mind if I borrow it?"

"Go right ahead, Mira." She handed her the paper. Kerrville just might be her best bet. She needed to get away from there. Away from home.

"Thanks. I'll go on up then. I appreciate it, Madeleine. I just need to sleep, and I'll feel a whole lot better in the morning."

"I'm a little worried about you."

Mira smiled. "Don't be. I've been through worse. I'll be fine."

She turned toward the stairs. "Oh, Mira, wait. I have something for you."

Halting, she glanced back. Madeleine rounded the desk and handed her an envelope. "The guy in 201—you know, the one with the caiman boots, like you said—he left this for you. Asked if I'd give it to you when I saw you. Here you go honey. Probably a nice little tip. I wanted to make sure you got it. I'm sure you can use a little extra cash right now."

Mira felt the tears welling up as she looked to Madeleine's outstretched hand. The white envelope with her name scrawled across it was blurring second by second. She snatched the envelope and shoved it into her back jeans pocket.

"Thanks, Madeleine," she said. "I'm sure it will come in useful."

She stumbled toward the steps then, trying not to let the woman see her cry. She hated crying.

A tip. A goddamned tip for the chunky hotel maid. Thanks for the fuck honey and go out and buy yourself something pretty.

Well, no thank you.

As she slid the card key into the door at room 201, Mira was barely inside and had thrown the deadbolt when the full-blown sobs hit her. Angry at the world, and especially at Jake and her Pop, she let her duffle bag slam to the floor and threw herself on the bed. Crying herself to sleep had never been a thing she had allowed herself to do, ever—even after her mother had passed. But she had no choice in the matter tonight.

Tears consumed her until exhaustion set in and finally, she fell asleep.

Chapter Nine

"Can you stick around this afternoon Jake? I have a delivery coming for the kitchen—your mom's new appliances—but I need to check on another job about that same time." He ticked his head toward the two men hanging out on the back porch. "These guys run a few bricks shy of a load. I can trust them to stay on task while I'm gone, but I have no faith that either one of them would make sure the delivery is correct. It sure has been nice having you around the past few days since things got sidetracked. Can you do that for me?"

Jake took a sip of his coffee and nodded. "Sure thing, Cy. You have a list of what's coming?"

"Yep. Right over here."

Jake watched his childhood friend cross the kitchen toward the butcher-block island and grab a clipboard. He'd known Cylas Branson since grade school and could see why his parents entrusted the remodeling contract to him. He was a pro through and through.

It had been a little over a week since he'd moved into his parents' house to help oversee the remodel and he liked to think he'd been a big help to Cy. He'd stayed longer than he had intended but the work had gotten delayed when two of Cy's guys quit to go work for another contractor.

His friend handed the clipboard to Jake. "It's all here. Refrigerator. Range. Dishwasher. Trash compactor. The deliverer called earlier and said he'd be here between one and four. Thanks for hanging around. I really appreciate it."

"No problem, Cy. It's not like I have anything else to do."

"And far be it from me to point out that you've been a real sourpuss the past several days."

Jake rolled his eyes. Literally. "Yeah, well. That's life."

"So, what you gonna do about it?"

"Nothing."

Cy sneered. "I'm gonna whoop your ass boy. You need to go call that girl and figure things out."

Jake shook his head. He'd told Cy too damn much. Why he did that, he didn't know but he guessed he'd needed to talk to someone. Probably it was the bourbon. "She's not interested. Besides, I can't find her. I called the hotel. She's not working there anymore."

"You know where she lives. Right?"

"Wrong. I even swallowed my pride, went to her house, and talked to her father. He said she'd moved out the night he sent me on my way and told me, again, to keep my hands off his little girl."

"Like most any father of a beautiful young woman would do when in the presence of a rogue like you."

"Cut it out, Cy. I've chastised myself for days. I've tried everything I know to try to find her. No luck. She doesn't want to be found."

"Does she know how to get in touch with you?"

He thought about the envelope he'd left with the front desk clerk. Surely, the woman had delivered it to Mira, hadn't she? "Yeah. Pretty sure she does."

Cy inhaled deep and studied him. "Well, I got nothing else. Sorry, but I gotta run, man. Call me if there's any trouble with the delivery."

Jake nodded. "Will do. Be safe."

Cy left and Jake pulled his cell phone out of his pocket for the third time that morning. No text messages. No missed calls. She really wasn't going to call him. Was she?

Mira sat in the passenger side of truck as it jostled over the gravel road. She bit her lip and stared out the window, then reached for the pile of paperwork fluttering about on the dashboard in the big truck cab. The guy in the center of the seat knocked her elbow as she grasped the papers.

"Sorry Mira," he said.

"No worries."

It was just the three of them in the truck. Her, the guy in the middle, and the driver. They'd made four deliveries this morning and had two this afternoon. This one was the farthest away from Kerrville and she had to wonder what time she'd get home tonight. She was supposed to register for an online course by seven. She hoped she made it.

She'd lucked into getting into summer school—just made the cut-off when she'd gone by the college four days earlier. Luckily, they still had most of her paperwork on file and she only had to update a couple of things.

She'd landed this job at the big box hardware store the next day. She was three full days into her training.

Studying the countryside, she had an inkling of where they were going but she had to be certain before they pulled up to the house.

"This the next drop off?" she asked, picking through the invoices and pulling off the top one.

"Yeah. Last one for the day."

"That's what I was thinking."

Mike, the driver—a big burly guy about Chandler's age—nodded toward the back. "We got big pieces to off load with this one, Mira. You can help us get them strapped up on the dolly but leave the heavy lifting and moving to us. Joe can show you how to operate the lift but don't touch anything. You're still in training, remember."

Mira understood. She was the new girl. Emphasis on *girl*. But she was grateful for the job. Working for the store in Kerrville provided her with flexible hours and time for taking her classes. She needed to do both, and this was the best bet. Besides, she liked doing something a little physical to keep her in shape. She was going to be sitting in a chair writing a lot for her classes.

"Got it," she said. "Hey look, I'll handle the paperwork, get the signatures, and all that crap. You guys do your thing. I won't get in the way. Deal?"

Mike dropped his chin. "Deal." He turned into a circular drive. "Here we are."

Mira glanced back down to the invoice, taking note of the name at the top of the page. *Jacob Remington, Sr.*

She sucked in a breath and looked out the truck window toward the house. *Jake's parents' house. Crap.* She'd wondered when they had turned off the main road but wasn't certain. She'd known his family lived on the other side of West Hills Ranch but had honestly never been back the long drive to the house.

Thank God Jake had left. He'd surely be back in Kentucky by now—it had been seven whole days since she'd last seen him—and no way his parents knew anything about her, so she was safe.

"Let's get this done," Mike said.

"I'll second that." Mira swallowed, lifted the metal latch on her door, and climbed down out of the truck. Gathering the paperwork and fastening it to a clipboard, she steadied herself and headed for the front door while the guys started doing whatever it was they needed to do in the truck behind her.

One step after another, she made her way up the two porch steps, crossed the wide veranda, and rang the doorbell. She waited while heavy footfall approached from the inside. As the door swung open, she blinked, sparks arcing inside her brain, making her suddenly light-headed. She stumbled a little.

The man reached out and grasped her elbow, steadying her. She'd had no clue how much seeing him again would affect her.

And seeing him really did affect her... Her heart slammed against her chest wall and her cheeks grew warm.

Mira whispered his name. "Jake."

"M ira...? Thank God."

Jake grabbed her before she could leave and shut the door behind her. Tugging her farther into the entryway, he repeated her name. "Mira. Honey. I can't believe you are here."

"I... Jake, look. This is a mistake. I didn't know you were here. I'm—"

"I don't give a fuck why you are here. You're *here*. And I'm not letting you leave until we talk." He would not look a gift horse in the mouth, and he was not the kind of guy to let happenstance go unnoticed. "Can we sit down? How about over here." He tugged at her sleeve and started to guide her toward the den.

She halted. "No. I'm working, Jake. Please."

"Please what?"

"Please just let me do my job. It's a new job and I can't screw this up, okay? Besides, we need to finish here so I can get home. I have things to do tonight, and we have appliances to deliver here today." She glanced at the papers in her hand. "Let's see. A refrigerator, dishwasher..."

All business. Was that all she could think about? Here she was, standing in front of him, acting as nonchalant as a paperweight and all he wanted to do was haul her up against him and kiss her. How could she be so damn cool and distant?

He took the papers out of her shaking hands. *So, she wasn't as collected as he thought.* "Fuck the appliances, Mira. Please, let me explain some things."

The doorbell rang again.

Mira glared. "That's my co-workers. Is this the best way to bring the stuff in here? Which way is the kitchen?" She turned on her heel and headed away from him.

Jake blew out a short breath and stalked after her. He rounded her and opened the door, shooting a sideways glance her way. He was not letting her get out of this house before they had a chance to talk.

He nodded to the men. "Yeah. Through here is great." He watched the two guys roll the dishwasher in on a dolly. Mira gave him a sideways smirk and followed the two into the kitchen. Jake followed along behind her like a lost puppy.

Dammit. That's how he felt. Lost.

Jake bided his time while the men unloaded the dishwasher and Mira checked off some boxes on the paper. "You'll need to get your plumber out here to hook up the dishwasher," she said. "We don't do that."

"Duly noted," he told her. "Coming in the morning."

"Great. Sign here for this one." She shoved the papers toward him. The guys sidestepped them and headed back out to the truck. "The refrigerator is next," she added.

Jake didn't care about the fucking refrigerator. He handed her back the paperwork. "Mira, look," he began again. "I want to explain why I walked away the other day."

She stared straight at him. The cool look on her face was almost more than he could stand. Did she not feel anything anymore for him? Had she gotten over him so quickly? Shit. If so, he was in trouble.

Finally, she spoke. "I know why you walked away. It's a man thing. My Pop. You. Man code. Yada yada. I get it. No worries."

Jake narrowed his gaze. "Then why are you pissed at me? Why haven't you called me? Hell, you barely look at me right now."

"Pissed? What makes you think I'm pissed? And how would I call? I don't have your number."

"I've tried to reach you, Mira. I've left messages everywhere. Asked you to call me and left my number everywhere, but you haven't. All I want is a chance to talk to you again. Dammit Mira, I can't sleep and I can't function. I've barely eaten. I need you."

She laughed nervously. He could tell by the crack in her voice. That gave him a little hope. Then her expression grew a little more somber.

"Look Jake," she began, "I don't know where you left messages, but I've not talked with anyone. I've been in Kerrville the past week trying like hell to get my life together, so I've been busy. And I'm steering way clear of the West Star and the ranch. Secondly, what in the hell do you *need* me for, anyway? To make your bed? Clean your bathroom? Shine your boots? Be your beck and call girl? No. Not happening."

She glanced off and crossed her arms over her chest, then said quietly. "Not enough tip money in the world for me stoop that low."

Jake stared. "What?"

"Tip money. You know exactly what I mean."

"What the hell are you talking about?"

"The money you left for me at the hotel! You know, for the *maid.*"

"What the fuck are you talking about?" He shook his head. "I didn't leave you any tip money, Mira."

"Sure, you did. Madeleine gave it to me at the front desk. I can't believe you did that. After finally getting over that chunky maid shit I was starting to trust you again. Then you leave me with my father. And the final blow? A tip for services rendered. Do you have any idea how awful that made me feel? Like I was a common whore or something."

Jake waved his hands in the air. "Whoa, whoa, whoa. You've totally got the wrong idea here. And I have no clue what you are talking about."

She squared herself, perching her fists on her hips. "You left me a goddamned tip in an envelope and gave it to the desk clerk."

"No. No." He shook his head. "No. I didn't give her any money."

She stared. "No, you gave her an envelope with money in it."

Jake huffed out a breath. "Hell, Mira. No. I gave her an envelope, but it didn't have any money in it. What the hell do you think of me, anyway? I would never..."

"But Madeleine said it was tip money..."

"Well, she was wrong. Do you still have the damn envelope? Did you even look in it?"

She shook her head. "No. I..."

Her gaze played over his face for a few seconds, then she shoved her hand into her back jeans pocket and pulled out the sealed white envelope. "I guess I left it in my pocket. Good thing I haven't done laundry yet this week." She stared down at the crumpled envelope. Jake noticed her hands were still shaking.

"Open it," he said softly. "Please."

She pulled at the flap, and then lifted her gaze to meet his. Those big brown eyes of hers were exhausting. He wanted to bury himself in them. And her.

"Go on. Look in the envelope, Mira."

She did. He watched her slide out his business card. "Oh God, Jake. It's your card?"

Nodding, he said, "Yes. Turn it over and read what it says on the back, honey."

Mira sucked in a slow, easy breath. "Please call me. I love you." She whispered the words, and then slowly looked up into his face again, tears spilling over her lower lids. "Oh, Jake. I'm so sorry. I love you, too."

She paused and slowly lowered the paper in her hands. Jake watched the expression on her face soften from irritation to compassion in a second.

"Jake," she whispered. "Why did you leave me like that at my dad's? Why would you ever think you're not good enough for me?"

His eyes closed against the words he didn't want to hear—or say—and his head lowered. But he had to tell her. Now was the perfect time. He lifted his gaze and moved closer. Grasping her forearms, he said, "Mira, in my youth and hell, even recently, I've been pretty much irresponsible with women and I've gained quite a reputation. A bad reputation. I never did anything illegal but there was a paternity lawsuit and... Well, I'll admit. I love women and lots of them. But all of those women...?"

"They're in the past?"

"Permanently. In the past." He nudged closer. "I swear, Mira. You're more woman than most men can handle but you're damn perfect for me, and all I ever want."

She lifted her chin and grinned. "I told you once before, Jake, I don't care about what you did last week, or in the past. The past is the past. All I care about right now is the future."

Grinning himself, Jake wrapped his arms around her back, holding her close to his chest. "The future? A week ago, you said all you wanted was the one night. So that's changed?"

The right corner of Mira's plump red mouth jerked up. "Yes. That's changed."

Mira's breasts fell into his hands, unleashed, and he relished the sexy fullness of them in his palms. After Jake had dismissed the workers and ordered the delivery men to leave the appliances on the porch—he'd figure out how to get them to the kitchen later—he lifted Mira into his arms and carried her up every step in the staircase to his room and peeled her clothes off her inch by achingly painful inch. Once they were both fully naked, he couldn't get enough of her skin and flesh in his hands.

Mira's head fell back as she leaned into him. He clasped her tits tight, squeezing and pressing her back into his chest. He bit softly into her shoulder and raked his mouth up the column of her neck.

"Oh God, Jake..." Mira hissed. "Don't stop. Ever."

Quickly, Jake turned and walked her backward to the bed. She sat and leaned back; he grasped the threads of fabric on her hips to pull off her thong and toss it aside. Then, following her down to the bed, he placed a hand on either side of her shoulders.

"I'm going to fuck you silly, woman." He growled and Mira giggled.

"Fuck me until tomorrow comes."

"And when tomorrow comes, I'm going to take you home with me."

Mira stilled and stared up at him.

Jake drew back. "What?"

"What do you mean, take me home with you?"

He smiled. "Come to Kentucky with me, Mira. Let me show you the other side of me. Who I really am. You can come back to Texas if you don't like it, whenever you want, but I swear, honey, you're gonna want to stay. You're gonna love it. And me."

Mira wrapped her fingers around his biceps and leaned up to kiss him. "You're a big talker, Jake Remington. Pretty damn full of yourself."

"Why, yes. Yes, ma'am, I am." He grinned and she smiled back.

"I already do, Jake Remington."

He arched a brow. "Already do what, Mira Featherstone?"

"Love you."

"To Kentucky and back?"

She grinned. "Yes. Maybe just to Kentucky. Period."

Jake leaned in, softly kissed her lips, and whispered. "I want nothing more, honey, than to take you home with me and keep you there forever—but I need to be sure that you're sure too. I want you to be very, very sure that being with me is what you want. Texas is your life."

Mira silenced him with a finger to his lips. "Texas was my past, Jake. I'm ready for my future. My life, I hope, is wherever you are. Anything else I need will fall into place."

"You're sure?"

"Why yes, sir. Yes, I am."

Jake grinned and then growled. "Then I'm going to fuck you silly, woman. And then I'm going to take you home and love you forever."

Mira smiled back. "Good enough."

Read on for the first chapter of ETHAN: BLACK SHEEP COWBOY, Book 7

ETHAN: BLACK SHEET COWBOY—Chapter One

"I hired someone to go over the books."

Ethan MacKay lifted his gaze from the cup of black coffee he'd been staring into and glared at his twin brother, Evan. "Why'd you do that? I thought we were going to tackle that together."

"To be perfectly honest, you're not tackling much of anything these days, and I have enough to keep me busy with the day-to-day around here."

Ethan frowned. "And I'm here to help with that too."

"Are you?"

Slowly, Ethan brought the now-cold coffee up to his mouth and took a sip. He held the cup with both hands to steady it because of the lingering tremor in his left one. His doc said that should lessen in time—it won't ever been perfect again, he'd added—but it was taking too damn long. "I'm getting there." *Give me a fucking break, man.*

"I don't want to rush you, so I'm taking one thing off both our plates right now."

"And I appreciate that."

"But there are things that need to be done, so—"

"So, you hired someone." Ethan stood, ambled to the kitchen sink, and tossed the cold coffee into it. "I get it." *And I thought we were going to make these kinds of decisions together.* He stood for a moment, bracing himself against the counter to ease the pain in his lower back and take the pressure off his left leg. Staring for a long minute out the window, he perused the South Dakota ranch he'd grown up on, and had to wonder why even after all this time it looked foreign. Then he mentally shook himself—it had been years. Too many. Ten, he thought. Maybe more.

The years were a blur.

He hadn't been there. His brother was used to making all the decisions. Why should today be different? *Besides, I'm basically AWOL.*

"We needed someone. Since I gave Grant Farmer the boot, the accounting books have sat untouched. Dad relied on Grant for everything, but we couldn't afford to keep him on as the ranch accountant."

"I can't believe you fired him. He was one of dad's best friends."

"Yeah, well. It was business."

"So, you hired someone else. Doesn't make sense."

"Yes. She's temporary and not nearly as expensive. And she'll be here about noon. Will you be around?"

She? Ethan turned back. "Of course. You know that, asshole."

Evan flipped him the bird. "And you need to fix that attitude. Get out of the house occasionally, man. Talk to people. Walk out to the barn and smell some shit or something. Better yet, go see Mom. You're spending way too much time alone playing those internet games."

Ethan smirked. He hadn't seen his mother since he'd been home, and he hadn't planned to do so until he was in better shape. No use having her worry over him any more than she already had. "Go play with your cows. I'll be here. And I'll get out to see Mom in my own damned good time."

"You said that last week."

"And you're not cutting me much slack here, brother."

"Did I ever?"

"Hell no. We never cut each other slack. And you know this isn't me. I just need to get my head wired back straight, let my body heal a little more. Just another couple of weeks."

Evan stood, hands on hips, and looked him over.

"What? Don't fucking look at me like that, man. Like I'm some weak, pansy-assed, pussy or something."

Evan laughed. "No one ever would say that about you, Ethan. Hell." His brother's smile faded, and his expression grew serious. "But I wonder if you need to check in with the VA in Ft. Meade," he continued. "You've been home a month, Ethan, and haven't left the house. You watch your coffee every morning until it turns cold, then you stare out that damn kitchen window for another hour. I wish I knew what's going on in that head of yours. Wish I had my brother back. We need you right now."

And I need you. More than I want to admit.

Ethan turned back to the window. Evan was right. His brother probably did need him. Their family was scattered right now, and that didn't help the situation. With their father dead, their mother a mess, and their three brothers and sister all off doing their things, who could blame Evan for wanting him to help pick up the slack on the ranch? After all, it was one of the reasons he came home. At least that's what he'd told himself.

But Ethan had problems of his own and Evan knew that. That's why he found comfort, somehow, in staring out over the brown and green rolling hills of Sweet Grass Ranch. It was something familiar in the world of chaos that his brain had become. What Evan didn't realize, though, was that at times, Ethan wasn't looking at South Dakota grasslands and cattle, but at the brown dirt of Libya, the desert of Afghanistan, and the war-torn remnants of Baghdad.

He was still sorting through a lot of shit.

"I'll be back," he said. "Just give me some goddamned time."

He heard Evan's footfall head toward the door behind him. "All right. Hey, when she gets here, just show her Dad's office. Crank up the computer there, will you? I think I have all the hard copy files laid out but make sure she knows that there are receipts and shit in the filing cabinet, too. Dad left things in a helluva mess. I'd ask Mom to come over but—"

Ethan briskly turned back to face his brother. "Let Mom be. I'll handle it. She's got enough on her mind."

Evan agreed with, "Yes, she does," and opened the back door. Looking out, he added, "I better get a move on."

Ethan closed his eyes, not ready to face seeing anyone yet but he guessed he had no choice. "Hope she's not some nit-picky, pain-in-the-ass old broad," he muttered, and headed for another cup of coffee. Maybe this time he'd even drink it before it got cold.

To ensure that, he pulled a bottle of bourbon down from the cabinet and poured half a shot into the coffee.

His brother slammed the door as he left. Ethan winced.

Brandley Mendoza swallowed hard and glanced into her rearview mirror at the dust billowing up behind her. It had been several weeks since she'd driven up this dirt road toward the main house at Sweet Grass Ranch, and truth be told, she never thought she'd be driving up it today. At least not to work. If it hadn't been for Evan MacKay's call a week ago asking for her help, she wouldn't have caved. But Evan had always been nice to her and his sweet-talking didn't hurt much either.

If she hadn't known any better, she would have thought he was flirting with her. Which would have been weird, since she was once married to his twin brother.

And that fact was what made her say yes. Eventually. She'd had to think on it for a while. But Evan and his family were like her own. Had been for many years and even though she and Ethan parted ways years ago, she kept in touch with the MacKay's and felt she owed it to them.

Especially now with Hap MacKay gone.

"I'm forever grateful for your help," Evan told her. "Just a lot on my shoulders right now."

She nodded. "I'm sure of that, being the oldest. I know your younger brothers help but I also know they are busy with their own lives and careers. It's too bad Ethan can't dig himself out of some desert hidey-hole somewhere to come home and help you."

Evan's voice took on a stoic tone. "Ethan left to protect our country and I'm damned proud of that fact, Brandley. You should have been too."

She'd immediately felt remorse at her words, and purposely avoided his last comment. "I know you're proud of him, Evan," she said quietly, "and I meant no disrespect. Whatever bumps in the road Ethan and I had, he was always loyal to his country and his men. They came first, no matter what. Always." *And as a young teenage bride, I had a hard time understanding that.*

But all that was water under the bridge now, and there was no reason why she couldn't help the MacKay's in their time of need. That's what people did around here.

As she pulled up to the house and parked, Brandley doubted her reasoning—and her sanity. Even after all these years, approaching the main ranch house felt like coming home. There was a huge void in the pit of her stomach that ached with the nostalgia of it all.

That void was Ethan, and the life they could have had together. And today, for some reason, she was having difficulty shaking it.

But she was here now, and this was business. Hell, she could use the cash. She had a job to do, and she would just have to push any thoughts of the happy, earlier times with Ethan MacKay, and his family, out of her head.

She was a grown woman, now. Not a silly, love-struck teenage bride, in love with the idea of being in love. And in love with the idea of being Ethan's wife. The young girl who would have been perfectly happy barefoot and pregnant, and running the ranch from her perspective—from home and hearth. The kitchen. And the bedroom.

She'd wanted that like nothing else. And thought that was going to be the life she and Ethan shared—then Ethan joined the Navy.

She shook her head to rid herself of her thoughts as she exited her SUV and headed up the porch steps. She had work to do.

And seeing that she was not the kind of person to back out on a promise, putting Ethan out of her head was what she had to do. Ethan MacKay, the black sheep of the family, was long gone from her life, and she doubted she would ever see him again.

Brandley raised her hand to knock on the door but before her knuckles hit wood, it swung open. Evan stood in the doorway.

"Hi, Evan." She took a step. He stood solid in her way, blocking the entrance. Brandley glanced up. "Evan?"

No, wait. *Shit.*

Her heartbeat kicked at her breastbone. Her head swam. The hair—an overgrown military cut. His chest—too broad. His eyes? Full of determination and…pain? The tattoo on his forearm.

She leaned against the doorframe to steady herself. "Ethan?"

"Brandley."

She took a breath. "Oh my God. Ethan."

"What the fuck," he said, and turned and left her standing in the doorway. She watched him limp away.

He was trained to expect the unexpected, but Ethan had to admit that seeing the woman standing there on the porch only proved he was off his game. Petite but shapely, long black hair trailing down her back, eyes dark blue as a Dakota night sky—eyes that widened when she'd realized it was him standing in the doorway. And of course, he certainly hadn't expected to see her again, his ex-wife, standing on the other side of his front door.

Yet, in the back of this mind, he always knew that coming home meant the probability of their paths crossing. Eventually.

He inhaled and held the breath, then let it out slowly. "Yes. It's me, Brandley," he called over his shoulder, stopping and turning slightly. "Come on in and shut the door behind you."

She pushed off the doorframe, the interior door closed behind her. "My God. I had forgotten how much you and Evan look alike."

"Well, that's sort of a given for identical twins, isn't it?"

"Yeah, but I could always tell you apart by..."

Ethan faced her and exhaled. "Look Brandley. I imagine you are here about the books and want to know where everything is. Come on in. We appreciate your coming to help."

She stared at him and didn't budge. "I..."

He took a measured step closer and reached for her elbow. Hell. She looked good. "I'm not going to bite."

"Don't go there," she said, and finally stepped inside, passing him in the doorway.

Ethan chuckled to himself. Her brain always went to sex. And right now, sex was the last thing on his mind. He moved slowly to his left, toward his dad's office. "Everything's right in here."

He supposed she would follow. He didn't look back to check. Right now, his mission was two things. Get that damned computer turned on and point her to the books. Then leave. A good long session of staring out that kitchen window was in order.

Brandley. Hell.

"When did you get back?"

Evidently she had followed. He pushed open the office door and moved inside. Not prepared for small talk, he was for damned sure unwilling to get into a lengthy discussion about being home. And why.

"You're limping."

He ignored that too and rounded the desk to push the 'on' button of the old computer tower. Then he shifted to unlock the top drawer of the oak filing cabinet behind the desk. That accomplished, he pulled out the drawer, leaving the key in the lock.

Ethan turned back to face her.

The years had been kind to her. Her hair was darker, longer. And she was still in good shape, although maybe a little heavier. She'd been thin, but chesty back then, and he'd loved the swell of her breasts over her narrow waist. Her hips had always been full and womanly, and he had loved that. She wore a lot less makeup today than he remembered when she was eighteen, too. Still pretty, cute, with those dark blue, moody eyes. Fine crows' feet crinkled at the far corners. And she looked tired, especially around those eyes.

He wondered why.

Not my business. "Evan tells me there are files in the computer, and hard copy bills and receipts here on the desk." He pointed to the stack. "I suppose that's them. And more in the cabinet behind me." He ticked his head to the rear. "I'd say start wherever it makes sense, then let me know if there is something you can't find. I can't promise I'll have the answer, but I'll find out for you. Now, I'm off to get some coffee. Want any?"

Knowing he was abrupt, borderlining on asshole, he turned away. Ambling around the desk, his fingertips grazed the edges, steadying himself. Suddenly, his back was tired and so was his damned knee.

Brandley let out a long sigh behind him. "No coffee. I'm fine. I'll get to work. Thanks for the quick tour."

He nodded and kept on heading toward the door. "No problem." Slowly, but surely.

"You are limping," she said again.

"Yep."

"You okay?"

"I am."

"Are you home for good, Ethan?"

He halted. "I'm home for now." Hell, in his world, nothing was for good. Ever.

Get your copy of ETHAN: BLACK SHEEP COWBOY today!

ABOUT MADDIE JAMES

Maddie James writes to silence the people in her head—if only they wouldn't all talk at once!

From flirty contemporary romance to darker erotic titles—often mixed with a dash of suspense or a hint of paranormal—James pens stories that frequently blend a variety of romantic sub-genres. The happily-ever-after, of course, is non-negotiable.

Affaire de Coeur says, "James shows a special talent for traditional romance," and *RT Book Reviews* claims, "James deftly combines romance and suspense." Maddie is the award-winning author of over fifty titles of fiction—from short stories to novels—and a Top 100 Amazon Bestselling Author.

Learn more at http://www.maddiejames.net.

Don't miss out!

Visit the website below and you can sign up to receive emails whenever Maddie James publishes a new book. There's no charge and no obligation.

https://books2read.com/r/B-A-IIV-MRGU

BOOKS2READ

Connecting independent readers to independent writers.

Did you love *Jake's Temptation: Remington Ranch*? Then you should read *Ethan: Black Sheep Cowboy*[1] by Maddie James!

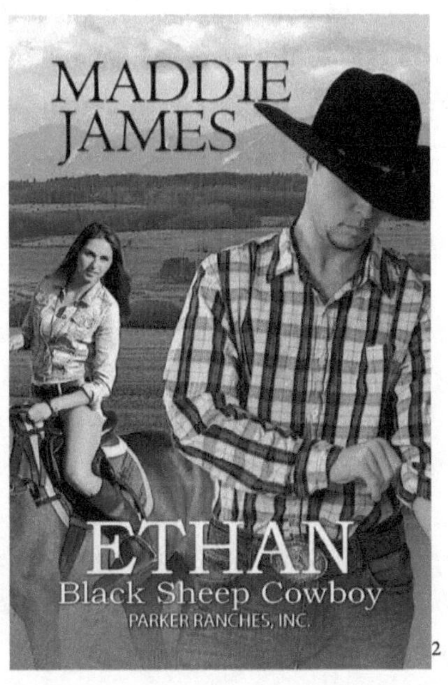

No one ever kissed her like Ethan. No one. And even after all this time, Brandley remembered his kiss—this kiss—like she'd had one every day since the day he left her.Navy SEAL Ethan MacKay returns to Sweet Grass Ranch to recuperate from an injury suffered on a mission, and eventually help manage the South Dakota family ranch with his identical twin brother, Evan. But he's been gone too long, and he's not the man who left the ranch over a dozen years ago. Not by a long shot. His body broken, and hopefully not his mind, he prays what they say is true—that cowboy runs deep in your blood—because this black sheep cowboy could sure use something familiar to hang his hat on.But being back home at Sweet Grass is

---

1. https://books2read.com/u/bWPx8G

2. https://books2read.com/u/bWPx8G

almost more of a challenge than heading up a special ops mission in Libya, especially when something familiar turns out to be the major challenge—**his ex-wife, Brandley Mendoza.**Brandley and Ethan's marriage quickly unraveled when he headed into SEAL training, and by the time of his first deployment, their relationship was fatally severed. Still, she keeps in close contact with the MacKays and considers them family. Hired by Ethan's brother to review the ranch's accounting books after their father's death, Brandley soon discovers Evan has an ulterior motive. Why he thinks she is the person to help Ethan get his head back on straight, she doesn't know, especially when she's dealing with problems of her own—namely, her ex-husband, who is seeking full custody of their daughter.But she risks coming down from her Black Hills safe haven to find out—only to realize that her heart is still vulnerable, and that Ethan isn't the cowboy she fell in love with when they were kids.*Can Brandley tease out the cowboy in Ethan's black sheep heart and rediscover the love they once shared? Can she resolve the issues of her own shaky past, to let herself trust again? Or are they both too far gone to even try?*

Read more at www.maddiejames.org.

Also by Maddie James

A Dickens Holiday Romance
Christmas in July
Charming the Prince

A Harbor Falls Romance
All of My Heart
Take My Heart
Dance into My Heart
The Christmas Nanny
Match My Heart
Tame My Heart
The Dating Game
Miss Matched Hearts
The Husband List
The Heartbreaker
Chase My Heart
Star Crossed
No Sweeter Match
One More Kiss
Not This Christmas
Perfectly Matched
Christmastime in Harbor Falls

Sweet Hart Inn at Harbor Falls: A Small Town, Second Chance
Romance
The Matchmaker Collection: Harbor Falls Romance Set 1, Books 5-9
The Matchmaker Collection: Harbor Falls Romance: Set 2, Books
12-14

Colorado Dreamin'
Rawhide & Roses
Broken
The Cowboy's Secret Baby

Holly Hill Inn
Home for Christmas
Miracle at Holly Hill Inn
The Last Christmas at Holly Hill Inn
Christmas at Holly Hill Inn

Seeking Witchdom
Witchling Summoned

The Forever Trilogy
The Forever Trilogy
His Forever Kiss
Her Forever Love
Her Forever Dream

The Parker Ranches, Inc.
The Rancher's Second Chance: Rock Creek Ranch
Callie: Rock Creek Ranch
Parker: Rock Creek Ranch
Corporate Cowboy: Branded Filly Ranch
Protecting Sarah: Branded Filly Ranch
Jake's Temptation: Remington Ranch
Ethan: Black Sheep Cowboy
Leaving Noah
Callie's Wedding
Rock Creek Ranch Box Set

Tuckaway Bay
That One Summer

Standalone
Tempt Me
Safe Haven
The Last Blue Eyed Woman
A Perfect Escape
Crazy for You
Convincing Nora
Double Crossed
Protect Me Not
Freshly Dead
Lost and Found
It's a Dickens of a Cookie!
Voodoo Bayou

Don't Tempt Me
What Doesn't Kill You
Colorado Dreamin' Duet

Watch for more at www.maddiejames.org.

About the Author

Maddie James writes to silence the people in her head. They finally quiet down when their stories are told. Author of 50+ romantic novels, novellas, and short stories, Maddie writes romantic fiction in contemporary, paranormal, and romantic suspense worlds. She's mighty partial to her cowboys.

Maddie began her romance writing career as a traditionally published author in 1997 and has published with several traditional and small press publishers. Currently, she works as an independent author publishing through her own imprint. Besides writing romance fiction, Maddie writes non-fiction under another name.

Winner of the Calico Trails Cameo Award (Roses & Rawhide) and the Romance Book Scene's Best Novella Award (Red: A Cajun Seduction Tale), Maddie has been listed as a Top 100 Contemporary Romance author at Amazon, and a Rising Star of Western Romance at iBooks. Affaire de Coeur says, "James shows a special talent for traditional romance," and RT Book Reviews claims, "James deftly combines romance and suspense, so hop on for an exhilarating ride." Read more at www.maddiejames.org.

www.ingramcontent.com/pod-product-compliance
Lightning Source LLC
Chambersburg PA
CBHW031742150726
47989CB00006B/2565